KILSHEE

Imelda Megannety

Kilshee

By the same author available on Amazon.co.uk

Song without words
Kaleidoscope
Her Sixth Sense
Return to Moineir
The Last Exit

Chapter 1

Nessa stopped at the village store and café and had a coffee. It was getting late, and she was tired and half asleep from all the travelling. She gave a prepared list of items she needed to Joe, the shop keeper and they exchanged pleasantries. He was used to her coming and going now. It was over two years since she had discovered this hide-away, completely by chance. It was the perfect place for an artist: off the beaten track, quiet, and the scenery, breath-taking. She sat and relaxed with her coffee as he set off to get the required groceries, throwing in a few comments as he moved around.

'I got Andy to bring a couple of bags of turf down when I heard you were coming. They are in the outside shed. Just shout when you want more.'

'I will Joe, and thanks. The place will be cold, I'm sure. When was it used last?'

'It's been empty since the end of August, so it'll be very cold and perhaps damp. There should be plenty of oil though. The agents in Killarney always have it checked out in between tenants and there's not many of them,' he chuckled.

She was looking forward to her old school-friend coming to stay for a couple of weeks. Although not constantly in touch, they were always able to take up from where they had left off, the last time they met. In many ways, they were kindred souls. Claire was a

1

quiet and non-demanding sort of girl. She was able to occupy and entertain herself, quite self-sufficient, Nessa thought. If she went off for a day's sketching, that was alright with Claire who liked to wander around in the woods or go off to the little beach, not far away, and loll on the sand, reading her book and swimming when she felt like it. She had also taken to kayaking. There was a small lake a couple of steps from the cottage. The shop at the beach rented out kayaks and Claire had become an enthusiast already.

They were well suited and had been friends for a long time. Like sisters, but better; no arguments about family or the empty talk that annoyed Nessa. Her own family was so argumentative, and it almost drove Nessa crazy. They could be lawyers she thought, all of them. Five brothers, all so loud and a father so quiet you would hardly know he was there. Mother of course, was the boss, the one who wore the trousers, as they said in Ireland.

The couple of boyfriends that Nessa had ever brought home, soon disappeared on meeting her brothers, who scared the hell out of them. She stopped bringing anyone home after that and none of them ever since met any man that she had an interest in.

Nessa said goodbye to Joe and took the prepared box of groceries that he had packed while she had drunk her coffee, and he gave her the key to the cottage, the estate agent in Killarney always left one with him. Being the only shop in Kilshee and being a small village, it was convenient for all. She settled back into the car just as the heavens opened. She hoped the weather would not change too drastically, she wanted to get a lot of sketches done before her return to London in mid-November. She was planning a Spring exhibition; that gave her four weeks here, all to herself and no distractions, she did not think of Claire as a distraction. Claire was a special needs assistant in Dublin and hated the hustle and bustle of the city. She told Nessa in July, that at the first opportunity she planned to apply for a job in the country, anywhere that was rural and away from the clutter of the city. She also loved to cook and that was a bonus as Nessa was hopeless and sometimes forgot whether she had eaten dinner or not. Her art consumed her, and food was always the last thing on her mind, until she realised that she was starving and would then look at the clock and be amazed at the time.

When Claire came in a week's time, they would both go and do a good big shopping and she would have a free hand in the kitchen. They would also indulge in the wine they both liked. Nessa knew that having Claire here, would enable her to work better and the company would be nice at night. There was no television or internet here and no reception for mobile phones which was how they both liked it. If they needed to use their mobiles or the telephone, they had to make the trip into the village five miles away.

3

It was raining hard now, and Nessa slowed slightly. The road was still not that familiar to her and she often missed the turn off to the trail in the woods and had to turn back. The road looked different too from the summer when she was last here. Tonight, was dark, and the driving rain made it seem darker. She looked anxiously out and tried to identify something familiar. There were no signposts or anything like that here.

After another ten minutes she knew that something was wrong. She should have reached the turnoff by now surely. She slowed further. Suddenly, ahead of her she saw a figure walking head down, coming towards her. Thank heavens, she thought. She slowed to a standstill and rolled down the window.

She smiled at the man in the heavy anorak and unruly red curly hair poking out from the hood and told him her plight. He was youngish and had a broad friendly face. He laughed and told her she was not the first person to get lost here.

'You have already passed that turn-off, I'm afraid. But not to worry, just keep driving for another couple of miles until you see a gap between the trees and a path to your left. That will bring you onto the trail you want, and lead to the cottage down by the lake. Just keep the woods on your left-hand, on the right there will be glimpses of the lake, you can't miss it.'

Thanking him profusely she drove off again. Imagine, she had passed the turn-off without realising it! She must be really tired from all the travelling. She would love to have just got on a plane and flown here, but she had all her art stuff to bring, so that meant the ferry. She had spent time loading up her car with the canvases and equipment she knew she would need and then set off. The traffic on the motorways on both sides of the Irish sea was heavy enough. It was now nearing eight o'clock and she longed for her bed. She would have to put on the heating of course, it would be cold in the old cottage she thought, unless it had been occupied recently, which Joe said, it hadn't. Not many people came here, she had been told when she learned of the property, and she guessed that was the reason it was so cheap and affordable.

At last she saw a gap in the trees and guessed this was the turn-off. Sure enough, after another couple of miles, driving at walking speed along a narrow and snaking path she met another path that was at once familiar.

Breathing deeply in relief, she continued now with confidence. There it was: the path to the cottage. Humming softly, she finally pulled up and got out. It was still bucketing down. Putting her head down she ran up the narrow pathway which in summer was almost overgrown with lavender and rambling roses. She reached the door and rooted in her bag for the key.

As she reached up to put the key in the lock, something knocked into her and pushed her against the door and then as suddenly, she was being pulled back down the path. She tried to look behind her but could not. Someone had his arms held around her and was pulling her like a sack of potatoes. She tried to put her feet back on the ground but could not. Her shoes then fell off and her heels dragged on the ground. She tried to struggle but it was hopeless. Then she was beside her car and the person holding her, held one hand over her mouth and nose hard, suffocating her. She was hurting and knew she was not strong enough to free herself. She tried vainly to free her mouth, but her arms were pinned to her sides. His arms were still around her and were as hard as iron, his knee digging into her back. As she lost consciousness, her thoughts drifted to her newly born niece. 'I'll never know her', were her last conscious thoughts.

Chapter 2

Claire pulled up in front of the cottage. She could see immediately that Nessa was out; her car was not there. It was a beautiful sunny afternoon even though it was cold. The narrow roadway had been covered in leaves and the whole of the small front garden was carpeted in the fallen leaves. She admired the colours as she took her luggage out of the boot.

She looked under the usual potted laurel for the key. There was no sign of it and Claire paused, puzzled. She put her hand to the door, but it was firmly closed. She wondered what she should do. She could of course sit in the car until Nessa returned. She put her luggage to one side and as she bent down, her eye caught sight of the key lying among the leaves.

Giving a sigh of relief, she picked up the key and let herself into the cottage. She thought it smelled of dampness and it was certainly cold enough.

Why on earth had Nessa not put on the heating? It never took long to heat the little place and they usually lit a turf fire, even on a summer's evening.

She brought her luggage in and then put on the kettle. Nothing like a cup of tea to warm one up, she knew.

There were tea bags in the tea caddy, and she brewed a pot. She looked in the basket by the fireplace; it was full of turf and logs. She searched and finally found an old newspaper, firelighters and matches and had the fire lit in a few minutes.

Now she was ready for the tea which should be good and strong. Going to the fridge to get the milk, she was shocked to find the fridge empty and worse, it had been turned off. She was more than puzzled now. It was not like Nessa not to have a fridge full of bits and pieces.

Looking in the food cupboard she found that it too, was like old Mother Hubbard's; bare, except for a packet of salt and a few stock cubes.

Suddenly she knew what had happened. Nessa obviously had not received her postcard telling her she would be delayed and decided to move to another location for the extra week. That was strange though, she always thought that there was enough to keep her busy here. Day trips were usually how Nessa moved to different locations. The village store was the usual place to leave messages. If only she had stopped there, Joe would have told her when to expect Nessa.

She carried her case upstairs to the bedroom in the loft that she usually used and again noticed how cold the room was. Coming back downstairs she went into the utility room off the kitchen and turned on the central heating and hoped that there was plenty of oil in the tank. As it rumbled into action, she felt reassured.

Claire got into her car to return to the village and talk to Joe and get some provisions to bring back. He would know when Nessa would be returning, in fact she would have left a message for her, and now she could plan a nice hot dinner to be ready for her return and a warm cottage.

Joe was surprised at Claire's request. He shook his head and said that Nessa had indeed picked up groceries two weeks ago but that she had not been in since.

'Oh, let me just ask the missus, she might have seen Nessa while I was doing deliveries.'

He opened the inner door and roared, "Mary!"

Mary came in and said hello to Claire. No, she had not seen Nessa but was there not some post for the girl?

Joe hit his forehead with his hand. 'I clean forgot about the post.'

He opened a drawer under the counter and rifled through it before closing it again. Turning, he reached up to a ledge behind him and pulled down a couple of letters and paper forms.

'Here 'tis.' He handed Claire the postcard that she had sent Nessa, explaining that she was delayed and would arrive about a week later.

Claire shook her head. 'Well she did not know I would be delayed. Where can she be, I wonder?'

Joe and Mary looked at Claire in bewilderment; the arrangements young people made, sometimes left them confused.

'Joe, I will try her mobile, it's only in the area of the woods and cottage that there is no cover.'

Despite dialling her friend's number many times, she got no answer. She wondered what she could do now.

'Could she have gone to her family?' Joe knew that Nessa was Irish and had a family here, even though she lived over in London.

'It's worth a try, Joe.' She sat down at the little table nearby and opened her address book.

Mary brought her over a cup of coffee. She smiled her thanks as she dialled the number Nessa had given her once. It was one of Nessa's brothers, the only one Nessa really got along with.

After a twenty-minute conversation with Niall, she finished with a sigh.

'No, her brother knows nothing but is going to ring the rest of the family. I will return tomorrow and ring him again. Maybe by tomorrow she will have returned anyway. I better get some supplies now and be ready.'

Joe helped carry out the box of groceries and told Claire to come in tomorrow anyway, to let them know if Nessa had returned or not.

Mary and Joe watched the girl drive away and then glanced uneasily at each other.

'Nessa is a sensible girl, Joe, no need to worry about her. These artists are a bit out on their own. She could easily just take a mad notion and have gone off somewhere without telling anyone.'

Joe did not give her an answer, he just stood at the doorway looking after the car.

As he stood there lost in thought, his son Andy came up the road.

'Well, and what have you been up to today, boy?'

Andy gave his father a cheeky grin and said, 'We were moving sheep all day, down to the lower fields. Most are in lamb now.'

His father grunted. 'I can't see why you would want to spend your life in a place like this. Farming! I mean, you could have trained in anything and got a job anywhere. I thought that work experience in New Zealand would cure you of sheep.' He shook his head and moved inside the store.

Andy smiled to himself and followed him in, taking a bar of chocolate as he passed into the house through the inner door.

His mother greeted him smiling. 'The hard-working lad returns. I have a lovely stew simmering for dinner, and I know you'll do it justice.'

Andy smiled at his mother. 'The way to a man's heart is through his stomach, did you know that Ma?'

Chapter 3

After a good night's sleep, Claire woke refreshed and lay in bed listening to the birds in the wood. This is the life she would love. She lay and thought about what it would be like, to wake up to the natural sounds of life in the country. The city was so frenetic, the traffic and noise so unrelenting, it drained the soul, she thought. It was difficult to get time to just dream and think. She had friends who lived out in the suburbs, those who were privileged to live in the more expensive parts of Dublin, in leafy quiet areas. She knew that she would never be able to afford a house or apartment there. Even if she could, would she want to live there? Every time she took a holiday in Ireland, far away from the city, she realised what she was missing. There were so many beautiful places she loved. It would be hard to choose, she thought. In the end, it would be her employment that decided. She loved her job as a special needs assistant and knew she excelled at it. If she could find a job in a place near the sea, with mountains too, that would be great. She wondered about an island existence once again.

She got out of bed and gave herself a severe talking to. She was lucky to have a job that she enjoyed and a family who lived nearby. She continued to chide herself as she dressed in a warm tracksuit.

She wandered down to the lake after eating breakfast and walked along the shore, recalling her kayaking experience in July. It was heavenly out on the lake. Nessa was usually too busy painting, so she was always alone there, not that it mattered. The peace and serenity of the place was totally relaxing, and she could feel all the tensions of work and life melt away.

At eleven o'clock she retraced her steps to the cottage and decided to head back to the village. She suddenly had a thought before doing this. Going up to the other loft bedroom that Nessa always took, she looked intently around the room. Everything was ship-shape. Not a thing out of place, not a tissue in the basket.

Going downstairs to the third bedroom, or Nessa's workroom and studio, she examined the room. Nessa was untidy to say it politely, there was always mess with Ness.

Looking around at the sterile room, Claire suddenly felt a jolt of fear course through her as she realised that Nessa had never been here, not recently anyway. There was no smell of oil paint or spirits, no discarded rags in the waste basket. Nothing! Now she was convinced: Nessa had not been in the cottage since arriving. So, where was she, where did she go? She then chided herself; there must be a perfectly logical explanation, Nessa was not totally unpredictable.

She drove thoughtfully to the village and sat outside the store for a few minutes thinking. She rang Niall's number while sitting there and hoped he would be home. He was a garda and could be anywhere. She was in luck; he answered. She spent a few minutes telling him of the situation here and of her belief that Nessa had not been in the cottage at all.

Then she remembered the key lying among the fallen leaves and told him about that.

He listened in silence. 'Well, the fact that the key was there at all, means Nessa must have been there, unless it was another key left by the last tenant.'

She told him the date that Nessa had picked up the key and groceries and the bad weather that had started that night and continued over the weekend, as related by Joe.

'That was two weeks ago, Niall. I am beginning to get worried about this. It is just not like Nessa at all.'

Niall thought it was strange, but knowing his sister, guessed that there could be a perfectly rational explanation. His sister was totally unorthodox in his view, look at her choice of career!

'Look Claire, give her a bit more time. If there is no word from her by Friday, I will drive down there.'

Claire sighed and agreed. It would be embarrassing if Nessa suddenly appeared and got wind of the worry she had caused. She was a free spirit after all and never had to answer to anyone.

Claire told herself that she was being silly to worry. Nessa was nearly thirty, for heaven's sake.

She got out of the car and went into the store. Joe was in his usual place behind the counter. When he was free from serving, she went over and told him what Niall had said.

'There is probably a perfectly logical explanation for her absence at the cottage and I'll just wait until Friday. What do you think, Joe?'

'I don't know Nessa as well as you do, Claire, but I would agree with her brother. Artists can be a little odd, shall we say? They exist on another plane, I think.' He laughed and shook his head. 'My Mary thinks so anyway, and she's got, what do you call it? Female intuition, that's what.'

Claire laughed. She picked another couple of items and a daily newspaper and left the shop.

She drove to the little beach where she had spent many happy days, swimming and just lying on the warm sand, reading her books. She was an avid reader and loved the long, uninterrupted holidays when she could indulge herself. The beach was deserted now, on this cold overcast October day. She could see from the village that the school children were all preparing for the weekend celebration of Halloween. It would be the same all over Ireland she knew. Pumpkins were decorated and put in the gardens of the houses dotted along the road. The beach shop was shuttered and would be closed now for the winter. The man who owned the shop had a sports shop in the nearest big town, about fifty kilometres away, where he also hired out kayaks. Claire knew that she would not be kayaking on this holiday now. She had considered it before she came. The lake was beautiful at this time of year with the backdrop of the trees in their autumn beauty. She thought of that poem they had learned in school, years ago, it was by Yeats, wasn't it? What was it called now? Yes, "The Wild Swans at Coole". She smiled, thinking of the nights by the turf fire at the cottage, drinking wine with Nessa and recalling and reciting those poems from school days. Nessa loved the poem: "The old woman of the roads" by Padraic Colum: 'O to have a little house! To own the hearth and stool and all!' They always laughed at this and imagined that it was this cottage the poem referred to. This would lead to discussions about how people lived in the past and the simplicity but hardship of their lives, compared to the ease and modern gadgetry of today's world.

It also made the women wonder about how they could cope with a life suddenly devoid of all these modern conveniences. That was why they liked being without communication with the outside world, albeit just for a short time. Of course, being near the village was the security they were not sure they could live without. It was the easy way of sampling olden day life they thought, without too much inconvenience or hardship.

After a brisk walk along the beach, she returned to the car and sat and read the paper, with the radio on. She then thought it was time to face the empty cottage, but her hopes again revived with the conviction that Nessa would soon be there too.

The day passed and there was still no sign or word from her friend. She was beginning to feel frightened now, what if her friend had an accident and was unable to call for help? Her mind conjured up all sorts of horrific scenes. She left the cottage and again drove towards the village where she knew she would get some coverage for her mobile. Pulling into a parking area outside the village school, she again dialled Nessa's number. Nothing. It was either switched off or the battery was dead. She felt helpless. She called her family for a chat and explained all that was happening. They were sympathetic and suggested going to the nearest police station and reporting Nessa missing. They also suggested that Claire should come home as soon as possible.

Reporting her friend's non-appearance to the police at this stage, was not an option, she felt. Nessa would never forgive this unwarranted invasion of her privacy if she suddenly materialised and had just been on a holiday. Anyway, she told them, Niall, her brother, was a guard and he was coming on Friday, he would know what to do.

Supposing she had gone to one of the many islands dotted around the coast? They had talked about doing that when they were here in July. The romantic idea of being on an island appealed to them both. They had spent many evenings looking at maps of local and nearby islands here, sitting by the fire and sipping wine.

She drove home slowly in the darkness and knew that tonight she would not be able to sleep so soundly. Something was wrong, very wrong.

Chapter 4

Niall tried ringing Claire's mobile on Friday morning without success, before remembering that there was no telephone or reception in their remote area. He then contacted the local station in Glencarr, the nearest town, to the village. He made his request and then proceeded to work for the last eight hours before his weekend off.

He was worried about Nessa but only met laughter when he mentioned it to his brothers. To them, she was one of the lads, well able to look after herself and a strong woman. She was flighty, that was true, liable to up and leave when the fancy took her. She had often gone off for days when a teenager and was always surprised and annoyed if people appeared upset by it. To her mind, there was always a good reason to do what she did.

Claire was alarmed to see a patrol car outside the cottage at midday, just as she arrived back from a walk along the lake shore. She felt sick as she ran forward to the garda standing beside it. He smiled and she relaxed.

'Hope I did not startle you, Miss, we had a call from Niall in Dublin. He has a couple of questions he needs answers to before he comes down here later.'

Claire sighed in relief. Niall was coming, thank heavens!

'About Nessa's car; is she still driving the old 'banger'----Niall's words, Miss, the old red Toyota that he gave her years ago? Would you know that?'

Claire thought quickly. Surely Nessa would have mentioned if she had got a newer car, or would she? She was so uninterested in cars or any material things, she might not.

'I think she probably is, she never mentioned getting a new car and perhaps she would, I'm not sure.'

The man nodded. 'The other question I was told to ask is: how long did she intend to stay?'

Claire thought hard. 'Well she did mention mid-November and she would have booked a return ferry, wouldn't she? She had planned to stay here about ten days after I left.'

The garda left soon after that and Claire went inside to have her lunch. She felt such relief that soon there would be someone to talk to about Nessa. What would she prepare for the evening meal, she wondered? There would be plenty of time before he arrived, she knew. She decided to drive all the way into Glencarr or the 'Big Town' as called locally, and get some provisions that Joe's store did not stock.

She felt much better with something positive to do and was soon humming as she tidied up the kitchen and made up the downstairs bedroom for Niall. The place was now well aired, and all the damp smells were gone. There was plenty of turf in the old shed at the back of the cottage that would keep the fire burning for a few days anyway.

It started raining heavily while she was in town. She packed her groceries in the boot of her car, hurriedly and started on the fifty-kilometre journey back.

She was nearing the village when she saw the man, struggling with a heavy sack and the rain pouring down. She passed and then had a pang of conscience and stopped. As the young-looking man drew alongside, she leaned across and opened the passenger door.

'Are you going my way, Miss?'

Claire said 'I am and this way to the village, right? You want a lift? Put your sack in the boot, there should be room.'

Without further ado, the man opened the boot and deposited his sack before gratefully getting into the passenger seat.

'You are very kind to stop for a stranger, Miss. I keep getting caught out in this sort of weather,' he laughed.

He pulled off his woollen cap and then turned his head to look at her. He laughed out loudly and startled Claire.

'Would you look at us? We could be twins, I'm thinking.'

Claire, glancing at him quickly, understood what he meant. They both had that fiery red, curly hair, often seen on this island.

She laughed too. 'We are proper Celts, we are.'

'You are a stranger in these parts. My name is Andy Cooney. I live in the village. My dad has the store there.'

'Oh, you must be Joe's son. Pleased to meet you. I'm Claire McKeogh. I'm staying at the old cottage in the woods.'

'That would not be so comfortable at this time of year, surely?' I know the place well. We used to fish in that lake and got the nicest trout you will ever eat.'

'Do you not fish there anymore?'

'Life is busy since I came back. I work on the farm up the mountains; sheep.'

'That's a hard life, I imagine, not very exciting for a young man.' Claire glanced again at him. He had a broad and friendly face and there was a relaxed and easy manner about him that made her feel relaxed also.

'When you say you have come back, were you away from the place for a while?'

'I spent three years in New Zealand, a wonderful country altogether: big, and the people friendly, underpopulated and they know their sheep.'

'Were you not tempted to stay, Andy?'

The young man paused before answering. 'There were certain obligations, shall I say, that made me need to return.' He sighed, 'I would recommend the country to anyone wanting a change of scenery. Speaking of which, their scenery is like ours, beautiful.'

Claire pulled up outside the store and Andy turned and shook her hand.

'Again, many thanks for the lift. I hope you enjoy your time here. Cheers.'

Then he was off and lifting his sack out of the boot. He gave her a quick wave before entering the store.

Claire drove home, with a light heart. How wonderful to meet someone you could chat with so easily. Andy was right, they could pass for siblings with that hair. In the rain her hair dissolved into long curly ringlets. She was jealous of those girls with straight hair but also knew that her friends were jealous of her locks. She smiled to herself, we are never satisfied with what we have, how true is that?

Now she had a dinner to prepare and hoped the gas canister was full. The oven was electric so that was alright. It would be at least after seven before Niall arrived. The roast chicken would be ready.

Chapter 5

They both enjoyed their dinner. Niall had missed the turn off and arrived late. He had been ravenous when he arrived, and Claire gave him a glass of wine and said they would eat first. She surveyed him as they ate. There was a strong resemblance to Nessa she thought; he was a good-looking man, very intense looking. They chatted easily in between the long silences. Both were thinking of Nessa who should be here too.

As they sat on the old, battered sofa, in front of the blazing fire, Claire felt her usual self for the first time in days. It was as if a heavy weight were lifted from her shoulders.

Niall put his glass of wine on the small table at his side. He took out a notebook and pen.

'Now to get down to business, Claire. Let's get all the facts down in black and white and see what we've got.'

They spent the next three hours going over every bit of information that Claire could provide. Niall's family did not have a lot of that. Nessa had let them know that she would be in Ireland over October and November and could expect a visit from her on her way back to London. Claire recalled every communication she had with Nessa since their last visit here in July. It was then that this trip was planned; it was a good time for them both, Claire would be on half term break and Nessa wanted autumn landscapes with all the various changes in colours to what she had painted in July. They had discussed a two-day break to one of the islands nearby.

Then it came to the night in question, when Claire had arrived, and she went over the whole scene again. She told him about her trip into the village store and talking to Joe and Mary. They knew the exact date that Nessa had arrived. Joe had packed her provisions and given her the key. No, Nessa had not confided her plans to him, so he was ignorant of her movements after that. She told Niall about the postcard that she had sent to Nessa but had not been collected.

'So, you see Niall, she had no idea that I was delayed by a week. I did not get any call from her in that week and assumed she had got my postcard. Then there is the funny thing about the key, it was lying on the step just in front of the door, almost covered by leaves. There was no trace of food in the kitchen.'

She did not have to remind Niall how untidy Nessa was. It was well known within the family.

Niall knew that there were only two possible explanations: Nessa changed her mind at the last moment to go elsewhere and dropped the key by mistake or else, she was abducted right here and he did not want to consider that.

'You are in a good position to dig about, are you not? I mean, you can find out things that I cannot.' Claire was beginning to think that Niall might not take the situation seriously.

'You are right Claire, and I have people checking up on a few things. There is an alert out for her car for instance. I sold it to her years ago and nobody in their right mind would buy it now, but then, you never know. There are enquiries at this moment going on countrywide, hospital admissions checked and that, also ferry sailings and cars registered both arriving and departing in the past month. The next thing we will have to consider is to issue an appeal about her whereabouts and put posters up with her photograph.'

Claire was relieved to hear all that and felt guilty that she could have doubted Niall and the family's concern. She was still worried in case there was a good reason why Nessa had not made contact.

'She could have had some sort of seizure or breakdown, couldn't she Niall.'

'If that is the case, someone will come across her.' Niall closed his notebook and finished his so far, untouched glass of wine.

'Sorry Niall, you must be exhausted after your day's work and all the travel down here. Your room is ready, and the heat has been on for a few hours now, so it should be cosy enough.'

Niall nodded. 'I am totally bushed, as they say. We will make more plans tomorrow. My brain won't allow me to think that far ahead.'

He rose and said good night to Claire. She cleared the dishes from the table and could not face washing them now. Tomorrow was another day.

She climbed the stairs wearily. Although relieved that Nessa's brother was now here, she began to worry again. Nothing had changed had it? Her friend was missing, and that word sent horrible ideas chasing through her mind. Missing women were usually found dead if they were found at all. On this island, small as it was, it had happened too frequently in the last few years.

She slept restlessly then awoke suddenly. What was that sound? Something has broken into her muddled dreams and she was now wide awake. She lay and listened intently but there was nothing further. At last, she knew sleep would not come again so she got up quietly and silently crept down the wooden stairs. The kitchen was bright enough with moonlight streaming through the windows. She took a saucepan out to heat milk for a cup of cocoa. As she straightened up a shadow momentarily crossed one window and she nearly dropped the saucepan in fright.

Rushing to the front window she peered out nervously. There was a sound that she could not identify, a swishing sound from the side of the house, near the old shed that used to house an old rowing boat. It was empty the last time they came, and Nessa sometimes used it to store finished paintings. She had already checked it the day after she arrived, and it was completely empty now except for a couple of sacks of turf.

She heard the swishing sound again. Someone was out there, but doing what, she wondered?

She timidly crept to the bedroom off the kitchen and tapped the door. There was no sound. She tapped again and called 'Niall'.

A heavy-eyed and tousle haired Niall emerged a minute late.

Claire whispered what she had seen and heard. Niall immediately put on the light in the kitchen, which had been in darkness. Hurriedly putting on shoes and a jumper he went to the front door and threw it open. The moonlit night was a boon, as there were no outside lights here.

'Who's there?' he called and went out.

Claire was terrified and wished he had not gone. She looked around and could see nothing to defend them with, except the poker by the dying fire. She grabbed it and went out after Niall.

He went all around the house, calling out every so often, 'who's there, we know you're there, come out.'

After circling the cottage twice and finding and hearing nothing, they both entered the front door again.

'You are sure you saw something and heard a funny sound? Niall was now wide awake as was Claire.

'I am sure, Niall. Something woke me and I couldn't sleep again, so came down to make cocoa. There was a shadow that passed the window and the swishing sound again.'

'Well, he's gone now, Claire, whoever it was. Could be a local busybody who has got wind of Nessa's disappearance and wanted to nose around.'

'Oh, don't use that word, please. That sounds so final.'

She began to cry, although she tried not to. It was as though she had been suppressing her tears all along and now that word, 'disappearance' had undone her.'

Niall cursed himself silently. 'Claire, I am so sorry, it just slipped out. Sit down and we'll have a cup of cocoa. Tomorrow we'll explore all over the place and please God, we will find something positive.'

He went and put milk in the saucepan that Claire had taken out.

They sat and sipped the hot comforting drink and Claire felt a little better.

'Tomorrow we will thoroughly search around the cottage, before we go further afield. I also need to speak to Joe and Mary. I never met them before, and I want a general background history of the village and its inhabitants.'

Claire nodded. It would be great to feel they could do something that would tell them where Nessa had got to. She felt a lot better with Niall there and was sure nothing sinister could have occurred in such a nice, sleepy little place.

Claire nodded off and came to, as Niall got up and took the cup out of her hand.

'Off you go Claire and try not to worry, we'll learn more tomorrow and I'm sure we'll find my wayward sister.'

They both went off to their beds and fell heavily asleep.

Chapter 6

Claire awoke and got the lovely smell of bacon wafting up to her room. Then she remembered the night before and got dressed quickly.

She found Niall in the kitchen setting the table for breakfast and found that she was hungry, even though she had a good dinner the night before.

'You were up early, considering the awful night,' she remarked as she came into the kitchen area at the end of the main room, where the cooker was.

'Sit down now Claire, and have a good breakfast, we have a lot of work to do.'

He deftly served her up a plate of bacon and egg and put several slices of toast on the table and a pot of tea.

'It's a long time since I had my breakfast served to me, Niall. It's like being in a hotel.'

Then ate in silence and enjoyed the simple but satisfying food.

Afterwards, when Claire had cleared and washed all the dishes from the night before and the breakfast things, she joined Niall outside in the garden. The sun was shining, and it was a mild day. He was going around the house again and looking on the ground closely.

Claire joined in. He did not say what he was searching for, but she imagined it would be footprints.

'We need to clear some these leaves I think, they could become dangerous, if it rains,' he said.

Claire went into the house and emerged with the sweeping brush. She began sweeping. The leaves were thickly piled all around the house and Niall went and dragged the dustbin from the back of the house. He started taking armfuls of leaves as Claire brushed them and deposited them in the bin.

It was warm work. Soon the path was clear. Niall stopped what he was doing and walked further down the slope at the side of the house. Crouching down he poked about in the leaves. Claire was glad of the break and leaned on the brush, getting her breath back. As Niall straightened up, she saw that he was holding something in his right hand.

Dropping the brush, she walked to where he was standing, looking down at what he had found. It was a brown shoe, a lady's shoe. They both stood in silence and Claire felt the blood drain from her face.

'That's Claire's shoe,' she whispered and again felt tears surface and blur her vision. She wiped them away with the back of her hand.

Niall looked at Claire and his face was pale and shocked looking.

'I can't believe this is happening,' he said in a cracked voice.

'Look again and see if the second one is here, Niall.'

They spend what seemed like ages, looking under the trees and under piles of leaves. They did not find the second shoe.

Niall told Claire that he would have to go and phone his colleagues and see if there was any news. As they drove in his car to the village, he turned and told Claire not to mention finding a shoe, not just yet. The less said, the better, he thought, and Claire thought that she understood why. If someone local was guilty of taking Nessa away, they would not be too worried if they thought that the newcomers knew nothing.

Niall sat in the car at the children's park area and made several calls. After thirty minutes he told Claire that there was no information from hospitals, ferries or car sightings, however, it was early days yet, he said.

They entered the store and after the couple of customers had been served, Joe came over to talk to Claire.

She introduced him to Niall and explained that he was Nessa's brother. Joe was looking worried when she said that Nessa still had not been in touch in any way with her family.

Mary came out and greeted Claire. She listened to their conversation and asked them if they would like a coffee. They said they would and sat down in the small niche off the shop. Joe asked Niall if they thought anything suspicious had happened to the girl.

Niall shook his head and said that he did not know and hoped not. He then asked Joe would he mind if he asked him a few questions? Of course, Joe was more than willing to help. Mary served the coffee and stood behind Joe's chair and offered her thoughts too.

Once again, Joe recounted the night Nessa had arrived with the torrential rain following. He even mentioned the provisions he had provided, the usual basics and a good supply of the chocolate bars that Nessa ate a lot of. They often sufficed for a meal when she was working hard, she had told him.

'Those Chocabite bars?' asked Claire.

'The very ones, took a whole box of them, she did.' Mary asked Joe if he told them about the postcard coming and never being collected. He nodded his head.

'Was there anything unusual happening that week, Joe? Any strangers around that you had not seen before?' Niall was reverting into his garda mode.

'Nothing at all. The children had just started their preparation for the half term holidays and the shop was a bit busier than usual, all the Halloween stuff being the attraction. It's not really tourist time, September is the end of that season really, although now and again a touring bus comes through with American sightseers.'

'I hate asking questions like this Joe, but is there anyone in the village with a criminal past or an inclination towards young unattached women?'

'There are a few odd bods, but nobody dangerous.' Joe now looked alarmed. 'You think something has happened Nessa, don't you?'

Mary, standing behind him, pressed his shoulder. 'I'm sure nothing bad has happened Joe, don't be getting upset love.'

Joe looked miserable. 'I always thought we lived in an ideal country, but over the years, bad things have happened. Oh, not in this village, don't think I meant here. But in other places and some not far from here, well you know what I mean. There have been a few cases of girls going missing over the years.'

Niall knew what the man meant.

'In one way, I am glad our daughter is living in New Zealand. It seems a more law-abiding country somehow. Our son Andy loved it but decided to return here.'

'These things happen in every country, Joe,' said Niall quietly. 'It's the times we are living in, I suppose. Where is your son living?' he asked. 'Are you training him to take over the business?'

Joe laughed dryly, 'Not at all. These young men have their own ideas, and he is working on a farm since coming back home. He worked on a sheep farm in New Zealand and that is what he likes.'

'Where is the farm, is it local?' Niall asked.

Mary said brusquely, 'indeed it is. His uncle's farm, three miles from here. His uncle owned a lot of land here, if you stand up by the children's park and look to the right, well, all that land was his uncle's.'

'You speak as if his uncle is dead, Mary.' Niall rose from the table.

'Yes, my brother died, and his wife now runs the farm with her brother.' She gathered up the coffee cups and walked over to the counter.

Claire felt that the interview, if you could call it that, had now ended. Niall thanked Joe for his time and told him that he would be there for the weekend and would probably call in before leaving for Dublin.

They drove home in silence. Claire remarked that Mary had sounded angry about her son working at the farm.

Niall explained how land was so important in Irish life and how the Irish fell out over land more than any other thing, especially when it came to inheritance.

'You might steal a fellow's wife and get away with it but take an inch of his land and he'll come after you with a shotgun.'

Claire laughed and said that it was a strange state-of-affairs for sure and wondered if it were only in Ireland that it happened. Then she got serious again, thinking of the incident the night before.

'Niall, someone was definitely prowling around the house last night. What was he looking for, do you think?'

Niall answered her in a quiet voice. 'I think he was searching for Nessa's shoe or shoes. Maybe he had one and couldn't find the other.'

Claire turning it over in her mind, believed that he was right. Whoever it had been, was looking for something specific. That frightened her, it meant it was someone nearby, maybe local who knew the area. She shivered and suddenly felt more than scared: petrified.

'Niall, I have heard that serial killers often take things belonging to their victims, trophies, they call them. Have you heard this too?'

'Yes, I have. I just don't want to think in that direction, Claire. There is a profiler already involved in several missing women's cases. It's a horrible thought and I pray and hope there is nothing like that involved here.'

Chapter 7

Niall decided to go to the large town of Killarney. It would take a couple of hours and Claire asked if she could come too. She was nervous about being in the cottage and Niall told her that she should return to Dublin, there was nothing she could do by staying here. She did not agree and felt it was her duty to stay and try and find Nessa. She could be somewhere close by, in trouble maybe; perhaps she had some sort of accident and lost her memory. All these thoughts swirled round in her head almost non-stop. Eating with Niall and having a bit of company was the only thing that kept her calm right now. She did not want to think of tomorrow when Niall would return to work in Dublin.

Niall had contacts and colleagues in Killarney and needed to chat with his own sort badly. He was very worried but did not convey just how worried he was to Claire. Why cause her any more anxiety than she already had? He knew he could access data there and put in his own findings and all the information they had already received. There was an excellent detective unit there.

The journey passed and Claire tried to keep some conversation going, to distract herself.

They spoke about their jobs and their families and even managed to laugh when they recalled the mad exploits of Nessa as a schoolgirl and then art student. She had been quite wild.

While Niall was in the station in Killarney, Claire took herself off to see the sights and do a bit of shopping, it helped to keep her mind off things.

She had lunch in a little café. She knew Niall would be eating with his pals and they had agreed to meet back at the car at around five.

That night back at the cottage, Niall again asked Claire if she would return home and again Claire said she would like to stay around for a while. Niall was going to try and get some holiday leave and thought that under the circumstances, there would be no problem. He needed to speak with his family who did not realise what he suspected. He wanted to be there with them and put them in the picture. At the same time, he did not want the gang descending on this small place and frightening the natives.

He left first thing on Sunday morning after issuing Claire with orders to take sensible precautions.

'Be inside once it gets dark, Claire, and keep the front and back doors locked, all the time Needless-to-say, do not open the door to anyone, even if you know them. They can convey what they want to say through the window. I also want you to report to me every day, say about eleven o'clock every morning, then I won't have to worry about you.'

She promised him to do that. He also had Joe's number and intended to ring him regularly.

As she sat having her solitary breakfast, she decided she would take herself off and go to the various local spots where Nessa frequented. The weather was autumnal and chilly in the morning and evening, and a fire was now not just a luxury but a necessity. She brought one of the two sacks of turf in from the outside shed and refilled the basket at the hearth. She thought she should get some more.

She set off to a spot above the beach where Nessa spent a lot of time painting and sketching seascapes. She parked the car and got out and took a brisk walk, breathing in the salt air. She then stopped and looked down at the beach where she had often swum. It looked so idyllic and peaceful. The sea was calm, and the waves gently lapped the shoreline. She thought that if a mild day came, she might risk getting in again. She recalled the paintings that Nessa had done when the sea was not so calm. They were so exciting and dramatic, she remembered. As she walked around the area, she found herself looking down at the ground. What did she think she was going to find, she asked herself?

She had lunch at the cottage and then drove into the village. She needed more milk and dropped into the store. Mary was behind the counter today and smiled warmly at the girl. She invited her to have a coffee with her and Claire agreed. There was a young girl behind the counter today too. Mary told Claire that she was being trained in.

'It will be nice to have an extra pair of hands. The weekends are very busy and being in a village, they expect you to stay open late. They're quite spoilt.'

Mary was chatty today. She asked when Niall would be back, and Claire told her he hoped to return soon.

Claire asked how Joe was and Mary sighed.

'I am worried about him. He suffers from blood pressure, you know, and he is also an anxious sort of man. He worries about everybody and everything.'

Claire nodded. 'It might be just his personality, Mary. Some people worry and some don't. He should have a hobby. Does he do any activity that he enjoys?'

'Well, he loves to fish. Himself and Andy used to go off a lot, especially in the summer evenings, but then Andy went off to New Zealand and the shop got busier and busier.'

'Well, Andy is back now, so why don't you encourage them both to go off like they used to?'

'Poor Andy is worked off his feet up on the farm. He is usually tired out by the time he gets home in the evening. They take advantage of his youth and vigour, so they do.'

To change the subject Claire asked about Mary's life and background. Did she always live here in the village?

Most people in this village had lived within five kilometres of the area. A lot of the inhabitants were related too. The school was full of first and second cousins. Mary had moved from the farm she was born on, to the village when she met Joe who was from a smaller village further south. Joe was considered very enterprising to buy the rundown and decrepit building that passed as the shop. There had been a pub attached to it but to renew the licence was too exorbitant a price for Joe and he just concentrated on groceries and a smaller hardware shelf. The coffee machine was Mary's idea, she proudly told Claire. She made jams and apple tarts too as apples were plentiful.

She told Claire how she missed her daughter and longed to see her again. The airfare to New Zealand was impossible for them right now. They had borrowed heavily to enlarge the shop premises and add an extension to the small house adjoining the building. She was not a complainer, she told Claire, but she missed her girl and was proud of her at the same time. She thought that she did the right thing in moving away.

Andy was a good son, she said, but a mother needs a daughter to chat to. Joe and Andy had a delicate relationship. Joe always thought that Andy could do better for himself than work up at the farm.

'But it was your home place, wasn't it, Mary? How long is your brother dead?'

She was told that he died a couple of years after the marriage. There had been a farming accident involving the tractor.

Claire nodded sympathetically. Farm accidents in Ireland were so common and even though more and more safety precautions were brought in, they still happened.

After that, her sister-in-law, Margie, told them she would run the place herself and her brother would help her and made it clear that she did not want any interference or help from the members of her husband's family. This of course, brought about a lot of ill-feeling. The farm was big enough to support more than one woman. Mary and Joe both thought that one of her younger brothers should have been brought into the arrangement.

'Does she have children,' enquired Claire?

Mary laughed bitterly, 'indeed the one she has is incapable of tying his shoelaces or anything else. He is not normal, Claire, and she never even tried to get him seen to. He doesn't talk. I think that's why Andy likes it up there. Young Paddy follows him around everywhere like a puppy and gets so excited each time he sees him, so he tells us. Mary knows that her son will never be capable of running the farm and when she or her brother dies, who'll look after it and Paddy?'

Claire thought the answer was obvious. 'Surely she will give the farm to Andy then?'

43

Mary sighed. 'You just don't know with those people, what they're planning. Andy might spend all his best years, hauling and heaving and working day and night and get nothing. It's not like you can talk about things like that here.'

'Why ever not? I think it would be the most natural thing in the world Mary, to talk about the future of the son and the farm.'

'Agh, things like that are complicated here and people prefer not to talk about them. There is enough bad feeling here and the area about, people never liked her family and particularly her brother who now runs the place. They were a strange lot.' Mary finished her coffee.

'It's a pity about the little boy, they should have done something, maybe he could have been helped.'

'Little boy? Sure, he is a big strapping fellow now, very strong altogether, he is a couple of years older than Andy.' She laughed as she got to her feet. 'Andy says Paddy could pick him up and throw him over a hedge, no bother.'

Chapter 8

Claire drove home, with a newspaper and fresh milk. It was still bright and early enough and she felt unsettled. She thought she would explore a bit more today.

There were wooded trails all over the place and today she parked in an unknown one. It was bigger and denser. She did not think that Nessa would have been here, but there again, maybe she had been. After all, she was not here every time Nessa had been at the cottage.

She put on her walking boots and was glad after fifteen minutes of walking. The undergrowth was wet, and the leafy paths bogged down in mud in places. It was a steep pull up the hilly area. Trees were packed close together and there were lots of old branches strewn on the ground, the results of high wind and storms she guessed. She loved the crunch under her feet on the parts that were dry. She stopped now and then to catch her breath and look around. The colours were dazzling. The path opened out further up and she could survey the road, far below. As her eye swept over the scene, she found she could see where the cottage was. It was not entirely visible because of the woods surrounding it, but she could make out the roof and the lake right behind. This spot would have been perfect for Nessa, she thought. She continued to climb and suddenly she was at the summit of the hill. Now the land evened out a bit and there were not as many trees. She stopped by a fallen tree trunk and sat and had a rest. The ground look like bogland, dark and earthy. There was a valley sloping away from her and she could see a farm, with outlying barns. There was someone on a tractor and she could see sheep grazing, as far as the eye could see. It was a beautiful vista and was like something that Nessa might paint.

That must be the farm that Mary was talking about, she thought. Wow! It spread out over the huge area that she could see, and the fields stretched further way into the distance to the horizon.

There was a well-worn track to the right, which would be the way to the main road, she guessed. So that was how Andy got to the place. He would not have to climb up through that wood.

On her return journey, she stopped often and picked up any dried branches or sticks that she came across. They would make a nice blazing fire she knew. Then as she again stooped down, something caught her eye. There was something under a tree among the leaves. As she went forward, she knew what it was, and her heart lurched in her chest. It was a wrapper from a Chocabite bar. She picked it up and looked at it. It looked fresh enough. She put it gently in her pocket. She knew she was silly to attach any significance to it. It was a common enough wrapper, wasn't it? Still, her breathing was more rapid and there was a strange feeling fighting for room in her chest. I must tell Niall, she thought. She hurried down the rest of the slippery paths and was still breathless when she reached the car. She sat and took out her mobile to phone Niall. She had to put it away as there was no signal.

She drove quickly to the children's playground where she usually rang from. His phone rang out and the message service came on. Damnation, she could not leave this as a message. It sounded too trite, and she suddenly knew that Niall would think her a silly female, grasping at straws.

When she finally reached the cottage, there was a car outside on the laneway. Claire immediately felt nervous. Who could that be?

She drove past it and parked where she always parked, by the side of the cottage.

A man was emerging from the car and he raised his hand in greeting as he approached her. Claire looked at him quizzically. She saw a well-dressed man of middle years.

He stopped a few feet from the end of the footpath and introduced himself.

'Sorry if I scared you Claire. My name is Aidan Savage, I am a colleague of Niall's and he asked me to keep an eye on you. We met recently in Killarney and I know that he is worried about his sister and about you, just now.' He then held out a card that she knew was his identification card.

Claire stepped nearer and could see it was a garda identity card. Even so, she was still a bit nervous. Was she supposed to invite him into the cottage?

As though reading her thoughts, the man named Aidan told her that he just wanted her to know that there was discreet surveillance going on and not to be nervous if she saw him around the place. They were acting with Dublin and even if she did not hear about anything on radio or television, there was an investigation going on. He held out another card to her and told her she could ring at any time, day or night, if she heard anything new or felt frightened.

She suddenly felt confident that he was, who he said he was, and smiled.

'Would you like to come in and have a cup of tea?' she asked.

'Only if you feel comfortable. I know it's a shock to find a stranger on your doorstep, especially as your friend Nessa seems to have disappeared.'

Claire opened the door and led the way in. There was that word again, 'disappeared'.

'People don't just disappear,' she said as she went to put the electric kettle on. 'Something has happened to her or else someone has taken her, but she did not 'disappear' into thin air.'

He sat down at the kitchen table and agreed with her. Then he told her something that she did not know. There were ongoing investigations into missing women. The women in question were all from within ten kilometres of this village.

Claire stood still with the milk jug in her hand and stared at him. 'I never knew that and neither did Nessa. We might not have chosen this spot if we had.'

As she poured the tea, Aidan told her that five and possibly up to ten women, between the ages of eighteen and thirty had all gone missing in the past fifteen or more years. Their families had not been too concerned at first, except for the eighteen-year-old girl who had lived at home, but she disappeared almost twenty- two years ago. The others were only reported a few weeks after not being in contact. Up to now, there had been no trace found or any sightings anywhere in the country. Of course, it was possible that some had left to go abroad, but in most cases the friends and families did not believe this.

Claire listened to all this. She then explained that her friend Nessa would not be in constant communication with friends or family, but she would never pull out of an arrangement like the one she had made with her.

'Look, we do this regularly; Nessa comes over to paint and will look in on her family at the end of the trip. I work in Dublin and love the short or long holidays spent with her. We were in school together for all our schooling, primary and secondary. We are like sisters and get on well together. We know each other inside out. If she had changed her mind about this holiday, she would have told me.'

'Do you mind me asking Claire, does Nessa have a boyfriend here or in England?'

Claire paused, 'Nobody here knows this, so I would be grateful if you did not tell the family; Nessa did have a serious relationship a couple of years ago. They had planned to get married but sadly her fiancé died unexpectedly. She got over the shock but did not want the family to come crowding her. She would not have coped with sympathy.'

Aidan nodded. 'They don't need to know that now, Claire. So, there was no man or lover on this side of the Irish sea?'

'No, she was a free spirit and was totally self-sufficient. She said that if she ever felt drawn to a man, he would not stand a chance!'

They both laughed.

'What about you Claire? Anyone waiting up in Dublin for an attractive redhead?'

Claire shrugged her shoulders. 'I wish! It's difficult to meet anyone in a city, regardless of what country girls think. My work is all absorbing. I have had a few boyfriends and there is one now, but it's more off than on.'

Aidan rose to go. 'Remember that if you want to talk at any time or if you hear any sort of gossip that is suspicious, just ring me.'

Then Claire thought of the chocolate wrapper and took it out of her pocket. She told Aidan that Joe in the shop had packed a whole box of the bars in the provisions she had bought that night.

He took the wrapper and noticed like she had, that it was fresh looking and of course anyone could have dropped it. Still, he thought it was worth making a note of it.

'It's all the little items of information that sometimes bring about a break-through.'

All information on Nessa, now would be added to the files on the other missing girls, he explained. In a week's time, they would have to publicly announce that Nessa was missing and place posters all around. The reason they held off was that in a small place like this, the media would descend and that would not help the investigation at all.

Claire had guessed this already. She wanted to help all she could, and Aidan understood. He did not want her to put herself in any danger and must ring himself or Niall regularly.

Chapter 9

There were a few beauty spots that Claire wanted to explore. She knew that Nessa had often used them in her paintings. Somehow it made her feel closer to her friend when she visited places she had been. The place today would bring her above the sea again, on a wild and windy ridge. There was a panoramic view of the ocean and a small indent in the sheltered area where Nessa used to set up her easel. The seascapes she produced here were wonderful and sold well, she had told Claire. Today, Claire stood huddled in her anorak and woollen cap. It was not a day to stand around long. There was a path down towards the sea. It did not reach the sea but led to a lower viewing point. She scrambled down the steep path and found the area that Nessa called her own. It was more sheltered here and Claire stood and breathed in the salty air. The surrounding hillsides were dotted with the white forms of sheep, and she thought of the young man who wanted to spend his life with them.

She made her way back after a while and was nice and warm by the time she reached the top area again. She turned to get in one last view of the sea and headed back to the car. She was surprised how fast the time went. She remembered her promised phone calls to Niall and reached for her phone. There was a missed call. Probably Niall, she thought. She frowned at the number, then her heart somersaulted. Nessa's number appeared and Claire breathed a sigh of relief. Damnation! She checked for the date and time. It had been sent last night at eleven o'clock. There was no message in the box.

She could have cried with disappointment and frustration. Again, she dialled Nessa's number and there was nothing. It must be switched off, she thought. Maybe she needs to conserve the battery, wherever she is. Her heart felt lighter, and she dialled Niall's number. His message minder came on and she cursed softly under her breath. This time she left a message, 'Niall, ring me asap.'

Driving back to the cottage, she stopped in the village. Sitting in her car she dialled his number again.

This time he answered and said sharply, 'Claire, I was about to ring you. I just got your message.'

She interrupted him, 'Niall! Guess what? I had a missed call from Nessa on my phone just now. It came in when I was up at Sheep's Head viewing point. It was sent last night at eleven o'clock, no message.'

Niall could be heard breathing at the other end of the phone. 'Claire, this is intriguing, I don't know what to make of it though. I am coming down tomorrow. I will leave here early in the morning.'

Claire was elated as she got out of the car and went to get some fresh bread. She had better get some more bacon and eggs for breakfast. Joe was serving today in the shop. He smiled to see her again. She thought he looked a little flushed and hoped he was alright.

She could not keep the news to herself. She told him about the call from Nessa, smiling broadly. Joe was delighted too and called Mary from the house to tell her.

'What a pity that there is no cover out at that place. You could have solved the mystery if you had taken the call when it came.'

Claire agreed and told them that Niall was coming back tomorrow. She collected what she needed and as she paid Joe, she suddenly had an idea.

Mary and Joe, suppose I leave my phone here with you, in case Nessa calls again. You would hear it, wouldn't you? Would you answer her and ask her if everything is alright and tell her that I am here and that her brother Niall is coming tomorrow. If she tried to reach me once, she will do it again, I know.'

Joe looked at Mary and both nodded their heads together. 'Of course, we will. That's a good idea Claire. I have a good pair of ears on me, and I will keep it nearby until we see you again.

Life seemed good again to Claire and she practically skipped to the car.

She took some beef from the freezer and planned a casserole for the following night when Niall would be here. Then she remembered Aidan. Should she have rung him with the latest information? No, Niall would keep him in the loop. She sat having a cup of tea and thought about her friend again. Poor Nessa will be mortified when she discovers how many people were worried and looking for her. Then she thought of those other women who were still missing and wondered how the families coped.

Dusk was falling when there was a noise outside in the garden. Claire put down her book and stood up. She checked the doors, they were locked. She looked out the front window and could see a figure coming up the path pulling something heavy. He went around by the side of the house and Claire's heart began to thump in her chest. Was this the person who woke her up the other night? There was a knock on the back door. What would she do? She was trembling. She had been told not to open the door to anyone.

The knocking persisted, then a voice she knew called, 'Claire, are you in there? It's me, Andy. I need to talk to you please.'

She swallowed hard and asked him to go around to the front and she would open the window. She felt ridiculous, but she was obeying orders.

Andy appeared at the front window and waved at her. She timidly opened the window.

'Sorry if I scared you Claire, I just want a word with you. You may be able to help someone I know.'

'Andy, the gardaí have warned me not to open the door.'

'Sure that's alright Claire, I understand completely. It's just that Ma said you heard from your friend and that she will be coming back shortly No, this is about a different matter. Ma told me about your job. You are a special needs assistant, right?'

Claire nodded. 'That's right Andy. How can I help you?'

'My Mam said that you help 'artistic' children, but I think she means autistic children.' He laughed softly. 'I don't know if you can help, just thought that I would ask. No harm is asking, I told myself.'

'Hold on Andy, I am going to open the door and you can come in.'

When she opened the door, she could see Joe's old van parked further down from the pathway. As he entered, he asked with a grin, 'are you sure you feel safe with me here now, Claire? I think you would be well able to clobber me if needed.'

He sat himself down at the table.

Claire asked him why he had gone around to the back door instead of the front door and was told that in the country, people always went to the back door. They felt it was more mannerly that coming through the front door and bringing in mud on their shoes. Besides, he had brought her a sack of turf and put it in the shed.

Claire laughed and put on the kettle. 'Many thanks for that. Now who needs help Andy?'

'It's my cousin Paddy. He is like an eight-year-old child, but I think if he got a bit of help, he might be able to talk a bit better. We get on so well together, but it is frustrating for both of us and recently he seems to be making a big effort to communicate. It's impossible for me to know what he means though. I just wondered if you could suggest anything.'

Claire thought for a few minutes. They sat drinking their tea and Andy pulled out a couple of bars of chocolate from his pocket and offered her one. They were Chocabite bars. She told herself to relax, lots of people ate these, not just Nessa. She took one.

Andy started speaking again. 'It's Halloween this weekend and I am bringing him down to the village for a few hours, to see the kids dressed up and trick and treating. He doesn't get down here very much. His mother is very protective, and his uncle would have him work around the clock if he could. This week the uncle Mick is away for a few days and I thought I'd sneak him down and give him a few euro to buy sweets in the shop.'

'I will certainly see him and try and have a chat or at least try and access if I have any skills to offer.'

She was touched to see the care in Andy's face and knew it was important to him.

Andy's face brightened up. 'That would be marvellous Claire, I would really appreciate that, so would my mother. They don't mention that side of the family too much and there is distrust on both sides. I seem to be the piggy in the middle and I can talk to old Margie. The brother is a different matter. There is a queer streak to him. I can't make out if he is afraid of Margie or if she is afraid of him. I suppose lots of families are like that. There was no brother for me, only a sister and we got along most of the time, what about you Claire?'

'Oh, I have two sisters, the eldest one is married with a little boy and I have one brother who is the youngest and just started teacher training college. My other sister is two years younger than me and works in a bank.'

'I don't know how Niall is coping with this affair, I don't think either my parents or I could cope if something happened to my sister.'

'I know Andy, I am just praying that nothing *has* happened to Nessa.'

Chapter 10

Claire slept well that night and felt that things would soon be sorted out. After breakfast she went down to the shop to collect her phone and see if there were any more messages or if Nessa had called the previous night. She was disappointed to learn that the phone had remained silent.

'Never mind, love. If she rang once you can be sure she will ring again. Come and have a coffee with me. Andy told me that you will see Paddy.'

They sat and chatted and Lisa, the new girl behind the counter seemed to be doing well.

'Tell me about Paddy, Mary. When did you suspect that all was not well with him?'

'We never saw the poor child after my brother died. She would not bring him to the village at all and even now, she does her shopping in the big town. I don't know what she thinks we ever did, to deserve this cold treatment. Something must have caused it.'

Claire asked her where she should see Paddy? At the shop or out at the cottage. It would depend on where the child/man felt most comfortable.

Mary thought awhile. 'The shop and village will probably be busy with all the kids dressed up and trick-treating. I'm sure that is going to make him very excited, indeed, maybe too excited. What about if Andy drives him out to you after he's had his sweets and gone around a few houses. Andy knows him best so I will ask him.'

'Does Andy have his own car?'

'Lord no! He cannot afford one yet. Joe gives him the van whenever its free and sometimes Andy helps him with deliveries. Most kids in the country drive from an early age, especially on farms.'

Claire thought about the coming weekend as she drove back. Niall should be here shortly after lunch she guessed. She would put on the casserole to cook slowly.

Niall arrived mid-afternoon. He greeted Claire but she got a sense of negativity from him. After a cup of tea and slice of Mary's apple tart, he admitted that things were not looking as good as he wished. He had spent time in the station at Glencarr, before coming here.

Claire's face fell and he immediately reassured her that a lot of work was being done. He pointed out the missing shoe and the person who had obviously been searching for it. Nothing changes that, he told Claire, something had happened to Nessa, that was the shared belief among his colleagues and superiors. Not only that; it showed that whoever it was, was likely to be local and knew the area and was able to return after some time to recover the shoe. Whether he had tried to find it before Claire came or not, was something they could not know, and guessing was not an option. The missed phone call however, opened up a new road. It could mean that Nessa was being held somewhere against her will and had somehow got an opportunity to use her phone. This was the most significant incident so far. There was a search into the whole area and nearby regions for satallite coverage and Nessa's number had been forwarded to all relevant stations and Claire's number also.

His news did nothing to diminish Claire's optimism and good feelings about Nessa. He told her he would be travelling to Killarney tomorrow and might stay a couple of days. She understood and was grateful that so much investigation was going on.

They had the tasty and sustaining casserole. Claire told him about Andy's request, and he nodded absent-mindedly as he drank his glass of wine.

'Now, if you please Claire, I am going to visit Joe and Mary again to clarify a few points and to try and get Joe's take on other visits by Nessa. Something might occur to him that did not seem important, so I will have to poke and pry like a bloody surgeon. Sometimes I hate this job.'

Claire laughed. 'I quite understand. Sometimes I have to poke and pry too, when trying to help kids. I have to put myself in their shoes and try and see the world as they see it, to comprehend the problem.'

Claire cleared up while Niall changed into more casual clothing, a warm track suit and trainers. Then they headed for the village together.

The shop was busy, and they sat and had coffee and waited for Joe to be free. Mary sat with them and was eager to chat.

There were a few women who had become used to seeing Claire in the village and they greeted her warmly. Most of the villagers knew that she was waiting for her friend to turn up. They were unaware that Nessa seemed to have disappeared. Joe and Mary had been very discreet.

Mary was quizzing Niall on what methods the guards had of finding missing people. He was explaining the many procedures that had to be gone through before a person could be pronounced to be believed missing. Sometimes it did not take long, especially if the person was known to be suffering from depression, say, or had domestic problems or substance abuse problems. Mary nodded at all this. She could understand all that.

'Nessa certainly did not suffer from depression in my opinion. She was a very steady, well-grounded person in my eyes, Niall.'

'Well, she was certainly extremely independent and always was, Mary. She always went her own way having made up her own mind about things.'

Joe eventually came over when things got quieter. Lisa was there tonight.

Niall began by asking Joe about the key to the cottage. How long had he been the holder of the key; the number of past tenants, who was the owner of the cottage? Claire felt sorry for all the questions being fired at Joe. She also worried about his blood pressure condition. She was sorry now, that she had not warned Niall about that.

Mary was the one who had the most information it transpired. The owner of the cottage was a rather eccentric English gentleman who had lived for years there alone. He had come on a fishing holiday, seen the cottage up for sale and decided to buy it. He only left the place about four or five years ago and decided to return to the place of his birth. She heard later that he had met an English lady who was visiting the area here, and decided he wanted to marry her, and so he left. She felt he was hedging his bets as he did not want to sell the cottage. He had an estate agent in Killarney who managed the rentals for him. It was arranged that Joe's store would be the place where clients could pick up the key. Joe and Mary were only too happy to oblige.

'How secure would the key be here, Joe?' Niall asked.

'Oh, very. Nobody would know what the key was for or who it belonged to. It was always kept in the drawer under the counter and it's not as though many people came renting that place. Everyone wants access to the internet these days and mobile connection. It would only be an eccentric, like your man, who would want to live or stay there. Sure, the Americans want to be able to run a pile of technical stuff, even on holidays. Makes you wonder why they bother to travel so far when they need those gadgets all the time, doesn't it?'

'Or my eccentric artist sister,' smiled Niall sadly.

'You don't have to be an eccentric to enjoy peace and quiet. The cottage is in a unique spot. Nessa and I love it here,' objected Claire.

Mary leaned forward and touched her hand, 'Of course you do, love. Nothing wrong with that at all. It's fine for a holiday place for sure.'

'Who owned the cottage in the first place, Mary?'

'Its' a complicated story, that, Claire. My sister-in-law and her brother lived there for years. After the parents died and she got married to Hugh, her brother Mick sold the cottage and moved up to the old farmhouse and started working for my brother.'

'So, this cottage was home to Margie and Mick? What did the father do for a living? There is surely not much industry around here', Niall remarked.

Joe nodded, 'in those days there was a big fishing business, and a lot of men were employed in that. It was not a bad living, in those days.'

Just then their son arrived and looked over at the four people around the coffee table. Claire looked up and saw him and greeted him warmly.

Niall looked up and saw the man with the shock of red hair.

'Is he a relative of yours, Claire, your brother?'

Claire laughed and Mary smiled and called Andy over.

'Andy, this gentleman thinks you might be Claire's brother!'

Claire introduced Niall to Andy and explained who he was. Andy smiled and extended his hand.

'What is this then? A round table meeting?'

Mary explained that Niall was Nessa's brother who was a guard and here about Nessa's disappearance.

Andy looked startled. 'Disappearance? Sure, that is solved, I thought? Mam, you said Claire's friend was in touch and would be coming back shortly.'

Mary looked a bit uncomfortable and looked at Joe.

'Did you ever meet my sister, Andy?' Niall asked.

'Of course, I saw her around the place, lots of times, but never actually met her, except that night of the torrential rain. She had missed the turnoff to the cottage.'

Joe turned to his son. 'You never told us about that son, what did she say?'

'Oh, nothing. I just told her that she had missed the turnoff and to go on another couple of miles and she would come to the other entrance to the woods.'

Niall looked at him and asked how long he had spoken with Nessa?

'I'd say about one or two minutes at most, I was soaked, and it was bucketing down.'

'Where were you going?' asked Niall.

'Coming home from the farm, we had been busy all day and rain was not expected, otherwise I would have phoned Dad to pick me up.'

Andy turned to Claire. 'Is it okay for me to bring Paddy on Friday night, Claire? If you have company it might be better if we wait for another opportunity. Paddy takes a while to relax with strangers, especially men.'

Claire shook her head. 'Not at all, I will be alone as Niall is going away for a couple of nights''

Chapter 11

Claire was on her own again. She felt unsettled. She felt that nothing was being done to find her friend and she needed to keep busy. Niall had been in touch and it would be the weekend before he would return. She had driven along the coastline over the past couple of days and noted the number of small villages she had passed.

Everywhere the scenery was beautiful, and she stopped a few times to take photographs. While out, she phoned her family and tried to sound optimistic as she spoke to them. They could not understand why she was still there. She told them she was with Nessa's brother who was a guard, and she was helping to talk to people about Nessa. She knew she was telling them tall stories, but she was anxious that none of them would come down and demand her return. As soon as she finished that call, she thought that she had just solved her helplessness. She should be talking to people about Nessa and asking questions too. Where to start she asked herself?

She returned to the village and stopped at the store. Mary was serving coffee and Claire joined the queue for one. She asked Mary as she was serving her, if she ever saw Nessa speaking with anyone from the village or any other place. Mary did not, so that was a non-starter. Anyway, Nessa was not the sort to chat casually to anyone. Her art was that which drove her. After the visit to the village, she went back to the cottage to bake. She always found baking a therapeutic and extremely satisfying occupation. She was slightly apprehensive about meeting Andy's cousin, Paddy.

As she waited for the sponge cake to bake, she sat and made notes of various difficult pupils she had dealt with in the past. She knew that language was a big stumbling block. She had bought some copy books and pencils at the store this morning and hoped that Andy would not go home disappointed.

She thought of the man who could easily pass as her brother. What had brought him back from a satisfying job in New Zealand really? There was something odd about it all, she felt. Why was there no communication between the farm and the village? Margie had been married to Mary's brother, for heaven's sake.

The cake was out of the oven and left to cool before she would ice it and cut it into squares. Now what, she wondered?

She decided to visit the beach and have a brisk walk along the shoreline. Pity it was not milder weather, or she would brave the water. Putting on her heavy fleece and walking shoes she set off in the car.

The beach was almost deserted. A couple of people were walking with dogs. Claire greeted them as she strode past. They were finishing their walk, it seemed. She was alone walking towards the rocky promontory at the end of the beach.

She was getting nice and warm with the brisk walk and slowed down and looked for a nice flat rock to sit on to admire the sea. There was nothing as good as the sea to balance the problems on your mind, she thought. It was always there; a constant, though changing from one day to the next. Of one thing you could be sure, the tide came in and then receded.

She sat and stared vacantly ahead. A sudden sound brought her back to reality. Someone was sobbing quietly.

Claire looked around and could see nobody. Then she stood up and peered over a rock nearby. She could not believe her eyes. There was Mary, all alone and wiping her eyes.

Before she could stop herself, she had called out to the woman. 'Mary, are you alright?'

Mary looked up startled and then looked embarrassed, as if she had been caught out in something shameful.

'Don't mind me love. It's my time of life!'

Claire picked her way over the rocks and sat beside her. 'Mary, what is bothering you? I know it's more than that. Are you worried about Joe still?'

'No Claire it is something completely different. I just need a good bawl now and again and it would be impossible to do that in the shop or even in the village without everyone knowing about it.' She blew her nose.

'Well, I have a good pair of ears, Mary and I don't live here, so if you want to unburden, please feel free. It might make you feel better, my dear woman.'

Mary calmed now and wiped her eyes again. 'It's a long story and an old story now, Claire. Everyone else has forgotten my dear brother but me. I just come here to mourn him, especially now, on his anniversary.'

Claire listened silently as Mary poured out her grief that never seemed to go away. She could not burden poor Joe with her sorrow, or anyone else. They had been so close growing up. They had shared many confidences and poor Hugh had always come to her for advice and solace.

He had been a happy-go-lucky sort of lad and was pleased to inherit the father's farm. None of the other three brothers were that interested. When he met Margie, he was happy and contented and Mary thought that he had met his soul mate. They seemed happy at first and compatible. Then things changed and he became quite depressed and a bit distant with Mary. She had been busy with her own family and did not pay as much attention as she should have, she felt. Now she was left feeling responsible for not being there for him.

Claire hugged Mary and told her that we all have a life to live, and we do our best. She was sure that

Mary had been a great sister to Hugh and had nothing to reproach herself over.

Mary shook her head. 'It's not that simple Claire. There are things that I have never told anyone, not even Joe. Maybe they should remain in the past, it's just at this time of the year I imagine Hugh beside me and telling me to put things right and I don't know how.'

'Talk to me Mary about these things, maybe you will be better able to see things clearly, by expressing them out loud to someone.'

Mary looked at Claire and then nodded slowly. 'You most never say anything to Joe, understand?'

'Mary, whatever you tell me will not pass my lips, alright?'

After a few minutes silence. Mary told Claire about her brother. Hugh was the eldest son and the one their father relied upon. He was a responsible and serious man although he had a great sense of humour. He was perfectly content with his lot in life and tried to run the farm as his father had. He was hardworking and conscientious and caring. When his parents had passed away, he had helped his siblings as much as possible. Mary had left early enough after she had met Joe and two of the other boys had emigrated to Australia followed later by the youngest where they had lived all their lives. One was still alive and in Brisbane.

71

When Paddy was born, Hugh asked Mary to be his godmother and she had been delighted to do so. They did not see each other too often. Their lives were busy and then Mary had Andy. Her daughter was a toddler then, so life was full and tiring. Developing the shop took all their energy.

It was about six months before the accident that Hugh made an unexpected visit to the village one night.

Mary was tired out after a sleepless night with baby Andy, but she was happy to see her brother. By the time he had left again for home, she was not at all happy and her worries started there. It was apparent to her that Hugh was deeply unhappy. She had never seen him out of sorts before and was bewildered, until he told her the reason. His wife had become distant and cold. He had tried to do all he could and thought it was the effects of having a baby. He was patient and loving until the night she had stopped him coming into their bedroom and told him to sleep in the spare room. When he remonstrated, she told him that Paddy was not his son and she did not want him sleeping with her again. Needless-to-say, he felt as though he had been electrocuted and could not say anything he was so hurt. Over the next few days, he had tried to talk to her and asked her if she needed to see a doctor, only to be laughed at. He said that she had not spoken to him in weeks. He was a lonely and broken man, Mary said. She did her best to comfort him and asked if he would seek help from a doctor and see if anything could be done to help her. No, he would never do that, he said, People in this part of the world kept their problems to themselves. He begged her not to even tell Joe. He felt guilty, Mary said, even though he had been nothing if not a good husband.

Mary sobbed again quietly. Claire did not know how she could comfort the woman.

'Mary, have you ever sought help to deal with this grief? There must be counsellors in the big town, Glencarr, or Killarney, that would help. You are overburdened with this guilt. There is probably nothing you could have done anyway. He could hardly have thrown her out without every person in the surrounding areas knowing about it and by the sounds of it, he was too private and proud a man to face that.'

'I don't know Claire; I did tell him to go to a solicitor for advice and he told me that he would think about it.'

'What happened then Mary, did things improve?

'Claire, he died before I could talk to him again. My big fear is that he committed suicide. It's killing me.'

Chapter 12

Claire watched sadly as Mary drove away in the old van. It felt awful seeing someone suffer and not be able to help at all, but more so as Mary was such a lovely woman that Claire had come to care about.

Now she had to find the energy to deal with Paddy. Of course, Andy knew nothing about all this, like his father. It was a heavy secret that Mary had to bear.

As she drove back, she had a stab of guilt as she realised that Nessa had not been in her thoughts for the past couple of hours.

She iced the sponge and cut it into small squares, placing a little jelly sweet on top of each. She knew that they were the sort of cakes that kids loved and guessed that both Andy and Paddy would love them.

The day passed and at eight o'clock there was the knock on the door that she was expecting.

The room looked inviting with two lamps shining in two corners of the old open plan kitchen cum living room and the fire was burning brightly.

Claire welcomed them in and felt quite dwarfed by the tall man that was Paddy. Somehow, she had expected an awkward teenager. She had forgotten that he was a couple of years older than Andy.

She held out her hand and smiled warmly. 'Hi Paddy, I am Claire and a friend of Andy's. How are you?'

He took her hand gently and said a long string of unintelligible words. She nodded and pointed to the table.

'Would you both like a cup of tea and some special cakes?'

Andy said that a good cup of tea would hit the spot and that he liked the look of the cakes.

'What do you think Paddy, would you like to try one of those square cakes?'

Paddy was sitting down, looking eagerly at the plate of iced squares and looked at Claire.

'Please help yourselves lads.' She poured tea into the pottery mugs and brought milk from the fridge.

The cakes quickly disappeared and then Paddy leaned back in his chair and gave all his attention to Claire.

As she poured more tea for them, Paddy lifted his hand and gently touched her hair.

'Bitty,' he smiled at her.

Andy grinned, 'I think he means "pretty," he likes the ladies, don't you Pad?'

Paddy replied in a garbled way and Andy shrugged and lifted his eyebrows at Claire.

'Paddy, I'm a teacher and I'd like to talk to you, but I don't know if you understand me. Can we try a few lessons?'

She took the copy books and pencils on the table. She quickly drew a face and curly hair. Pointing to it she said, 'that's Claire', then pointed to herself she said, 'I'm Claire.'

She pushed the copy over to Paddy and gave him the pencil and nodded for him to do the same.

He understood and awkwardly holding the pencil drew a circle. He laboured putting in eyes and mouth and hair, his tongue over his lips. He was like a young child and Claire guessed his mental age was below twelve years.

He finished with a satisfied grunt and pushed the copy towards her. 'Ah me,' then pointing to himself he said 'Pah.'

Andy was delighted and clapped his hands. 'You're great altogether Pad, can you draw me now?'

Paddy did as he was bid and really went wild with the hair, which made them smile. Claire asked him who it was in the drawing and Paddy smiled and pointed to Andy beside him, 'dah Dee.'

They spent the next hour doing simple things like this, she tried drawing sheep and a tractor and things that Andy felt he would be familiar with. She made more tea and Andy chatted to her while Paddy carried on drawing. She did not want to tire the boy out with too much stimulation. He seemed happy to keep drawing and Andy chatted about the forthcoming Halloween parties in the village and how he would bring Paddy to a few of the nearby houses, wearing his scary mask and how everyone would know who he was and what a great bag of sweets he would receive.

Andy stopped drawing and beamed at them both. He pointed to himself, 'Pah monna', then he resumed his drawing. He was obviously following their conversation and relating to the mask he would wear in the village as Andy interpreted 'monna' as monster.

Then the talk turned to Niall and Nessa. Was there any more news, he asked?

Claire glumly shook her head. 'I am more than worried Andy; the whole business is now looking sinister. Hopefully, he will have some news on any progress the gardaí may have made. They will be issuing a statement on national television soon.

Andy shook his head. 'It beggars belief, that someone can just disappear into thin air. There have been a few girls that have gone missing from this county and the surrounding two. Most people think that sometimes people choose to 'disappear'. When life at home becomes unbearable, do you know what I mean?'

Claire nodded. 'That's the awful problem, isn't it? Suppose they have not done it voluntarily? I know Nessa, she would not have done this. Either she has had an accident or something worse has befallen her.'

'Have they looked for her car or alerted the public?' Andy patted Paddy's hand as tried to pull Andy. He was getting tired they both knew.

Claire smiled at Paddy. 'I think you have had enough for tonight lad, will you come by again? I'll get some colouring pencils for tomorrow night.'

Andy spoke softly aside to Claire. 'Halloween is on but after that it depends on when I can spirit him away again. They don't want him to go into the village too much. I suppose they are afraid he might become accustomed to company and get into trouble.'

Claire sighed, 'what sort of trouble would they expect the lad to get into, for heaven's sake? Does his mother not want him to get better or at least be able to communicate better?'

Andy paused a moment and thought that if it were up to her, she probably would. Claire urged him to persuade her to let the boy come down more often.

Paddy was at the doorway. He was staring at an old print in a frame. Then he started pointing at himself and mumbling his long unintelligible sentences.

Andy looked up to see what he was looking at. He got up and gently took the picture down and they both looked at it.

'What is it? Is it a local scene?' Claire had never even noticed the old prints on the kitchen walls.

Paddy turned to her and again spoke in his own 'language'.

Andy laughed, 'I believe it's an old photograph of the farmland.'

Claire went over and looked. 'I don't see the farm,' she said.

Andy then explained that it was land beyond the farm, there was a shallow valley surrounded by the mountains. The water from the mountains ran down into a lake in the valley. It was all bogland up there, he explained. 'We often cut the turf bordering that area. It's a handy place in summer for the sheep to get water.'

Paddy was still pointing and jabbering away. He obviously knew exactly where it was.

'Does he go there often?' inquired Claire.

'Never alone, Margie would be afraid of him going too near the lake, we don't know how deep it is and he doesn't swim, you see.'

Poor Paddy was getting frustrated and having what Claire could only describe as a childish tantrum.

Andy opened the door, 'come on Pa, we better get back home, or you won't be allowed out again. Remember the Chocabites you have in the van.'

Paddy suddenly clapped his hands and laughed loudly, 'Gokka ites' or something which sounded like that.

Claire heard the old van drive away and suddenly felt tired. If only she could ring Niall now and have a chat. She washed the mugs and cleared up. She took up the copy book that Paddy had been doodling on and looked at the drawings. There were other heads there now, a female and a male. Could they be his mother and uncle? She smiled to herself. There was something that looked like the van, a small car and another like an old jeep and something else she could not distinguish: a rectangular shaped box or figure. It was covered in small circles. Oh well, only Paddy would know what that was. She would keep this and ask him the next time they met. She knew that if only he had been seen professionally when he was a small child, he could have received some help.

How many people were there like Paddy around the country? She felt totally inadequate to help him.

Chapter 13

Claire drove into the village and stopped at the playground as she usually did to make her calls. First, she rang her family again, who wanted all her news. She tried to sound calm and natural. She knew they wanted her home and were worried about her. She tried to tell them that progress was being made and she would soon be home. Her sister asked if she should come down and Claire hastened to decline that offer. They all had busy lives in Dublin and anyway, what help would they be to her?

Then she rang Niall and he told her that there would be a televised broadcast the following week and would she be prepared to be shown briefly, to let the public know what sort of person Nessa was? She agreed of course. She asked about the mobile call and was there any help there? Niall thought it was early days but there were some people working on that end. There had been no sightings of her car or any of her belongings and her bank card had not been used since arriving in the country.

She sat in the car and felt all the old fears crowding in on her again. How long more could she stay and bear this, she wondered? As she sat staring out of the window, her eye caught something out of the ordinary. In the playground there was Andy, and he was pushing Paddy around on a roundabout type of playground accessory. He would be too big for the swings, she thought smiling. She left the car and entered the playground. There were no other children there at this early hour.

'Hello, you early birds! How are you up so early?'

'Margie is in bed with a bit of a cold. She has a bad chest. Mick is still in Dublin, so I decided to make the most of it.' Andy looked quite happy pushing Paddy around.

'Would you like some breakfast?'

'Thanks Claire, but Mum already gave us a big fry-up.' Andy wiped his forehead, 'Whew! This is heavy work, Paddy. I have to rest a moment.'

Claire had another idea. 'Would you like another session while you are both free?'

'I don't have the van this morning, Dad is doing deliveries.'

'No problem, you hop in and we'll be there in a jiffy. I'll just go over to the shop.'

When she returned, they were both sitting in the back seat and Paddy was smiling broadly.

As they drove the five or six miles to the cottage they chatted. Paddy leaned forward and took Claire's mobile from the front well of the car. He started pushing buttons and jabbering excitedly.

'Hey there! None of that Paddy. That is very rude. You mustn't take other people's mobiles.'

Andy returned the mobile to its place.

'It's alright Andy, there is no reception once we leave the village. Let him play with it.'

They had coffee and the remainder of the sponge cake at the cottage. Claire put out the colouring book and pencils she had just bought. Paddy set to colouring with eagerness.

He was neat and orderly she noticed, finishing one item before moving onto the next.

'Paddy, who am I? she asked, pointing to herself.

He looked up briefly and started colouring again. 'Ce'h' he stated.

Andy turned to Claire, 'See, I told you, he understands everything.'

'Maybe not everything Andy, but who knows?'

He pushed the colouring book away and pulled the copy book from the previous night and opened the page that he had been on. He studiously started on another drawing, another female head. Again, he went wild with the hair; it was bright red and so curly that Claire was immediately affronted.

'God, is that how I look Paddy? There was I thinking I looked kind of cool.'

Without lifting the pencil, he muttered in his funny way, 'Bitty'.

'Oh well, if you think I'm pretty, that's alright. What do you think Andy?'

To her surprise, Andy blushed. Paddy muttered again more loudly, 'Bitty'.

Claire got up and put on the kettle again. More coffee?

'No, actually we better get going as Mick might be home early afternoon and there is a load of turf to be offloaded from the trailer. He will be annoyed if it's not all stacked good and proper, when he comes back.'

'I will drive you back Andy, it's too far to walk and you have worked hard this morning already.' She smiled.

'If you don't mind Claire that would be great.'

Paddy was reluctant to leave the table. Claire handed him a new copy and the colouring pencils. He laughed loudly and grabbed them from her.

'Not so fast Paddy, you must thank Claire for the present. What must you say?'

'Ce'h tirvermon.'

'You are welcome Paddy, but you must visit soon again, okay?'

'Kay Ce'h.'

Andy directed Claire to the nearest entrance to the farm. It was further up towards the wood that she had walked through. The side entrance was hardly visible with all the trees on either side of the road. It was a winding and narrow path, wide enough for a tractor she thought.

It was a bumpy ride, and she was too intent on the track to take in the surrounding scenery.

'Is it all bogland, Andy?'

No, there are some good enough fields and land but there is a lot of bogland too, of course. Great place for sheep though, it wouldn't be any good for cattle.'

After a couple of miles, the farm appeared on the horizon. There were green-roofed barns around the place. The farmhouse looked old and decrepit looking.

'Where do I find the front door?'

'This is the old farmhouse, you must pass this and take the next right turn off the track, Uncle Hugh built a nice modern bungalow further along. Mick lives in the old house.'

It might have been a modern bungalow when it was built, Claire thought, but it was certainly dated now. It had never been painted and looked rather bleak in the middle of a field. It had a sad look, she thought.

She stopped the car around the back of the house as directed by Andy. He hesitated a moment and then asked her if she would like to say hello to Margie.

He disappeared, leaving her in the kitchen, which was surprisingly cosy with an old Aga cooker on one wall. She looked around her. It could be a lovely pretty kitchen with a little care, but seemingly, no one had ever cared enough to do anything with it.

She heard muttered conversation. Then the kitchen door opened, and a woman appeared in a dressing gown and slippers. She had a severe appearance and a discontented look on her face and shoulder length greying hair.

'Hello, I am Claire McKeogh from Dublin. I am staying at Lake Cottage for a while.

The woman looked at Claire and appraised her from head to toe. After what seemed a long minute, she held out her hand and said, 'pleased to meet you, I am Paddy's mother, Margie.'

Claire took the outstretched hand and gave the woman her warmest smile. 'I have met Paddy and we had a nice time last night, didn't we, Paddy? She turned to him where he sat at the table again with his copybook open, colouring his drawings.

He spoke without looking up. 'Dah's Ce'h, Mah. Hergabmebux.'

Margie looked from her son to Claire. 'Are you the teacher that Andy told me about?

'Well, not a regular teacher, a special needs assistant, Margie. Andy thought I might be able to help Paddy a bit.'

'And can you?'

Claire was a little taken aback at the abruptness of the question. 'I usually only help children with mild learning difficulties, Margie, but having said that, I may be able to offer a little assistance especially vocally, but I am not an expert by any means.'

Margie grunted and sat down beside the Aga.

'Can I bring Paddy down to see Claire for the next few days, she won't be here for much longer Margie.'

Margie inclined her head 'It won't hurt, I suppose, but I don't want him upset or distressed in any way, understand?'

'Of course not! There will be no stress at all. It will be conducted in a casual and relaxed manner, mainly using drawing which will help distract him too.'

Margie looked at her son and sighed. 'You will bring him down to the cottage, will you Andy? If it's raining maybe you could do it up here, Claire?'

'No problem, either way Margie. I have an extra couple of weeks off as I have holidays due to me and they must be taken before the end of the year. Sometimes the special needs assistants have to work extra hours or wherever they are needed.'

Andy nodded and told them that he would bring Paddy down when the morning chores were down if that was alright with Claire. She thought it would suit. After all, she was not going anywhere, was she? She thought of her situation and the fuss that was approaching with the television appeal and what might happen after that. She felt apprehensive in one way but cautiously hopeful as well.

She looked at her watch and said that it was time she was going. Andy thanked her again. She told Margie that she hoped she would be feeling better soon. Paddy was still colouring at the table and hardly lifted his head when she said her goodbyes.

Chapter 14

Claire slept fitfully. Her dreams were full of shadowy figures and she knew that Nessa was one of them, but she could not recognise her, no matter how hard she tried. Eventually she fell into a heavy sleep.

She woke after ten and was dismayed. She did not feel refreshed like she should, after such a long sleep, she complained to herself. She ate her breakfast hurriedly and drove out to ring Niall and see what further news there was. She parked in the usual place. There were a few children playing, some already in Halloween costumes.

She reached for the mobile phone in the well of the car and could not locate it. After much searching and turning out of her handbag at least twice, she sat and thought.

Then she remembered Paddy's fascination with it. Blast, he must have taken it! He really is a child, she thought. What should she do? Wait until the afternoon when Paddy might come? Supposing there had been some developments? That decided her. She started up the engine and headed in the direction of the farm.

It was a dry day, and the air was crisp. A nice day for a walk, she thought. But I need to get my phone quickly and ring Niall.

She drove on and parked around the back of Margie's house as she had yesterday. The place looked quiet and there was no sign of Paddy.

She knocked at the door and waited. After what seemed like a long time, the door opened. Margie seemed alarmed to see her standing on the doorstep.

Her face relaxed when Claire told her about her predicament, and she beckoned for the girl to enter.

The kitchen was cold today and Margie was in her dressing gown. Claire apologised for disturbing the woman.

'I'll look in his bedroom. It'll probably be there. He has a habit of doing this, you know. He is only a little boy really, though most people would not understand that.'

Claire nodded her head and said that she completely understood, and she did not mind.

After five minutes, Margie returned, the mobile was in her hand. She handed it to Claire and hoped that he had not damaged it.

Claire looked at it and laughed. 'No damage done, Margie. Boys are fascinated with all these gadgets. Did you ever think of getting him one with these games and things?'

Margie shook her head.

'It may be good for him; young children seem to have a great understanding of how they work. I've even seen babies pick up remote controls and point them at the television screen,' she laughed.

There was no reaction from Margie and Claire again apologised to the woman and left the house.

As she drove away, Claire wondered why she felt so uncomfortable in that house. Margie was a strange woman for certain. Never seeing anyone up there, would you not think she would be glad of a chat and offer a visitor a cup of tea, which would be the normal reaction to someone calling?

She continued slowly, her mind digesting the strangeness of it. Suddenly she was brought back to reality with a jolt. She had almost collided with a tractor that she had not seen turning off the track.

The driver swerved onto the verge and as she passed, she raised her hand to apologise. All she got was an angry glare from the driver. It was not Andy, so she guessed that this was Mick, the uncle.

Should she stop and get out and apologise? She decided against that and thought that she would give Andy an apology to give on her behalf.

She stopped at the shop and got a few groceries and a newspaper.

Joe was serving and there was a delivery van outside. He was too busy for a chat but waved to her and asked if there was any news? As she shook her head, she thought she saw a worried look on his face.

He called to the young girl, Lisa, and asked her to take over. Coming over to Claire, he asked if she would call in some night after nine preferably for a chat with himself and Mary?

She told him that she was free every night and would call in tonight unless Niall arrived back.

She stopped at the playground and took out her phone and rang Niall. It was answered immediately although he did not greet her.

'Niall, are you there? It's Claire, is there any news?'

She heard his breathing and then a slight laugh, 'Oh Claire, I hoped it was you. How are things? You alright?'

She quickly gave him a résumé of her days activities since he had left. She asked him if there was anything new and when he expected to be back?

He assured her that things were progressing albeit slowly and he would probably be another day away. There was a lot of searching and investigating old cases going on.

Claire felt deflated, he had not mentioned Nessa and if they knew anything about her whereabouts.

She drove home sadly and feeling in desperation. Why were they investigating old cases? What had they to do with Nessa?

It was just before eight before Andy and Paddy arrived at the cottage. It was colder today, and Claire was cleaning out the grate when they came.

How did the trick/treating go then? Lots of sweets Paddy?'

Andy grinned and said he had enough to stock a shop.

Paddy sat straight down at the table and pulled out his copy books and pencils from his pocket. 'Pah Monna, Ce'h.'

'Did you frighten all the people, Monster?'

'Here Claire, let me set the fire for you,' Andy said. She smiled at him and sat down beside Paddy.

'Now Paddy, we'll have a little lesson, shall we?'

Paddy muttered something.

Claire took a fresh copy book out and started drawing. When she finished her quick sketch, she took Paddy's hand and put it on her copybook.

'What animal have I drawn, Paddy?

'Da cah'.

'Nearly right Paddy, can you say 'cat'?' She emphasised the T. 'Look Paddy, look at my face.'

He looked at her and watched as she put her teeth together and sounded the T again, over and over.

'Now you try it Paddy.' She smiled and nodded her head.

Paddy put his teeth together and with her he tried to make the sound Claire made. There was some success.

Claire tried drawing a few farm animals that Paddy was familiar with and each time, corrected his sounding of it.

Andy had the fire lit and sat and listened as she went through the different words with Paddy.

Paddy had quite good concentration tonight, maybe because he was so excited with the activities in the village and Andy could see that the man was trying.

After some time, Claire made tea and took out some biscuits. When they had the tea and a break from the work, she again went over the previous words and pointing to each one, asked Paddy the word. Each time he made the effort and finished the word properly, they both clapped their hands and said how good he was. Paddy liked the applause and clapped himself, beaming all the while.

They left him colour a few more pictures and chatted about the weather, the work they were doing and a few generalities like that.

'What about you Andy, do you have any sort of social life here?'

'Oh plenty, Claire. There are lots of sports here in the surrounding towns and villages. I play hurling most weekends and we play against various clubs around. It's a very lively place, although you probably have not seen much life here. Five miles up is the bigger village of Knocknabó and most of us congregate there at weekends. There are a few good pubs too which we like. It's a great place for traditional music. Every Saturday night there is music in one or other of the pubs.'

Claire nodded. She knew of the great music to be heard in rural areas particularly.

'Would you like to come and sample a Saturday night, Claire?'

She looked startled at the suggestion. Looking at Andy with her mouth open, she tried to articulate a response.

'Andy, I just could not do that at this moment with my friend missing. It would be totally inappropriate for me. Ordinarily I would like it. Do you know that there is going to be a televised appeal for Nessa next week?'

Andy flushed red and apologised profusely.

'What an idiot I am. Sorry Claire I just forgot for the moment. You must think I'm a right fool.'

'No of course not. The whole business is surreal to me. I mean, there has been no sighting of Nessa at all since she arrived in Ireland, according to the guards, no sighting of her red Toyota car, no bank card used. What does that suggest Andy?'

Now Andy turned pale and bit his lip. 'I don't like the sound of that at all Claire. If someone stole her car, it would surely have been spotted by now, wouldn't it? I mean, it's not something you can hide easily; a car.'

Paddy pushed his copy across the table to Andy.

'Cah'.

Andy looked absently at the drawing and nodded his head, 'good man'.

Claire said 'Carrr,' and tried to draw out the ending of the word. She again repeated 'Ruh' a number of times and then the word car again.

Paddy laughed and made a good attempt at the word and again was delighted with the applause of the two people at the table.

It was quite dark now and Andy thought he must get Paddy home. Again, Paddy stopped and looked at the print on the wall. Now he pointed and said quite clearly, 'Seeep' and he was right, there were a few sheep to be seen there grazing. Andy shot Claire a triumphant look as he went out the front door.

This time there was no tantrum and they both went down the pathway laughing. Andy turned around to give Claire a last wave.

Chapter 15

Claire had not forgotten Joe's request. At nine thirty she locked the door and drove down to the village. She felt tired after the session with Paddy, but her interest was piqued with the lad and she could see progress.

Lisa was in the shop serving with Mary. It was a dark and wet night and Claire wondered how long they had to stay open. It seemed a hard life to her, to work all those hours and be expected to stay open until eleven at night. They should be more businesslike, she thought. If the public knew the shop closed at nine, they would make sure they got what they needed by then.

As she waited for Mary to be free, she was surprised to see Joe emerge through the door leading to the house and go over and close the shop door as the last customer left. He locked it and put the 'Closed' sign facing out. Lisa also looked surprised and was delighted to be told she could go home early tonight.

Claire was invited to go through to the house. She had only ever seen Joe and Mary in the shop. The kitchen was a big warm welcoming room if a bit untidy.

The usual Aga range was giving off good heat and Claire took off her anorak. Mary bustled around putting out cake and china. The tea was made and soon they were sitting chatting and discussing various things as was the norm in this part of the country.

Eventually Joe put down his cup. 'You'll be wondering why I asked you here tonight Claire. I just want to talk about us for a change, uninterrupted.'

Claire looked at the man who was so familiar but about whom she knew nothing. He still looked flushed, and she worried about his blood pressure.

'I am very concerned about your friend, Nessa, as I'm sure you are Claire.'

She nodded her head and bit her lip and hoped the tears would stay away.

'I am worried especially because you are unaware of our story, or at least, my story.'

Mary leaned over and patted his hand. 'Joe don't go upsetting yourself, it's all in the past, so it is.'

Joe put his hand over Mary's and nodded. 'In the past, yes my love, and not talked about anymore, alas.'

He started his story and Claire listened hard and tried to absorb it as there were many interruptions from Mary and meanderings, here and there.

The main gist of the story, Claire understood, was about Joe's niece, Elizabeth. He was her godfather and was very fond of the girl. She was only eighteen when she disappeared; no trace had ever been found of her. Her father, Joe's brother, had died of a broken heart and Joe's sister-in-law, suffered health problems ever since. It had happened twenty-two years ago. The girl had lived at home and been a wonderful caring girl, not the sort to go off with a fellow or anything like that.

Joe and Mary had lost confidence with the police and any time Joe asked about the case, he was told it was ongoing, 'whatever that means', he added.

'Where was she going or where had she been when she disappeared Joe?'

'Well, that's the mystery; she was at the school where she had just completed her education and had been decorating the hall with her friends for a graduation party. It was supposed to be held the following Saturday night. The girls all said good night and left to walk home, which, I can assure you, was the normal thing for them to do. Sure it was the safest village around, so it was.'

'Was she with the others all the time, walking home?'

'Elizabeth lived furthest away, off the main road and up a small lane which led to the house. There are other houses on that lane, and nobody heard or saw anything unusual. They were all visited and thoroughly questioned, I must say.'

'What did the guards think at the time, Joe?'

Mary interrupted angrily, 'The usual stuff; that she must have eloped with a fellow, they were just too lazy to think anything else.'

Joe hushed her. 'Mary, I'm sure they did their best, but what could they do with no clues or any information?'

'Yes, it was so upsetting for her poor parents. Then they mentioned suicide to them and that was the beginning of the end for her father, my brother-in-law, God rest him.'

Claire pondered the sad story. 'You told me before that a few women had gone missing from the nearby area. Are they not investigating all these and maybe including Elizabeth among them?'

'They don't exactly inform me of anything, or the family either. Her mother is ill now, and Lizzie was an only child.'

Claire's heart suddenly lurched. Joe obviously was connecting Nessa with all this. Could that be possible? Surely not. Then she remembered the visit from Aidan Savage, the detective.

'Joe, I must tell you something. A man, he was a guard but in plain clothes contacted me last week. He was waiting outside the cottage and is from Killarney. He told me that Niall was in touch and that both Dublin and Killarney are investigating all these deaths, so Joe, don't give up! He sounded as though he knew what was going on.'

Joe and Mary looked stunned.

'Maybe you should not say anything about this to anyone here Joe. If it's a local person that is involved, the less that is gossiped about, the better. Don't you think so?'

Mary and Joe looked at each other. Joe nodded his head. 'I feel a bit of relief then, knowing that something is being done and that it is at last, being treated seriously.'

Claire could see Joe become more relaxed and Mary too. Then the kitchen door opened and in came Andy.

He looked surprised to see Claire there and smiled at them all.

'What is this? A meeting to discuss the village politics or just a friendly chinwag?'

'A friendly chinwag, Andy. Did you get Paddy back on time?' Claire smiled at the now blushing Andy.

'Yes, indeed and he was full of chat driving home. Not that it was all understandable, but he is busy sounding out those letters. I think it is working, you know?'

'There is no reason why he could not learn to read simple words, I think. Of course, lots of people don't believe mentally impaired people understand anything but I disagree.'

'I agree with you there Claire. I knew a man from way back, like a child he was, but let me tell you, he knew exactly how much change to expect in the shop and when it came to figures, he was nothing short of a genius.'

Mary laughed. 'I know who you mean, Joe. He was also very fond of the ladies.' She giggled like a schoolgirl.

Joe laughed and hugged his wife. 'Well I rescued you from your over-eager admirer, didn't I love?'

'Well, I never heard about that Dad, who was he, this admirer?'

'It's better that you don't know, son. We don't gossip in this house, do we?'

Suddenly Claire was yawning and could not believe the time; it was after midnight. Where had the time gone?

Mary saw her out to the front door of the house and walked across the road with her to her car.

'Thank you for coming tonight Claire. I think it did Joe a lot of good talking about his niece. He keeps too much to himself.'

'Mary, it was my pleasure. Mind that you keep an eye on Joe's blood pressure, won't you?'

'Indeed I will! He's due for an appointment at the hospital later this month. They'll do a whole range of tests on him, so they will.'

Chapter 16

Claire left a lamp on in the kitchen and ascended the stairs to her loft bedroom. She was exhausted and her brain was full of thoughts about the story that Joe had told her. She did not want to spend the night thinking about that.

She was asleep almost as soon as her head touched the pillow. Morning came too soon, and she lay relaxed and wondered what day it was. Time seemed to have stood still for her here.

She put on her dressing gown and made her way downstairs and put on the kettle. She would have a shower first and then have breakfast, she thought. She went into the modern bathroom that had obviously been added onto the older house. It was an electric shower, and she enjoyed the instant hot water.

She towel-dried her hair and immediately heard a knock at the door. Putting on her dressing gown she went into the kitchen and looked out the front window. There was Niall on the doorstep.

'Boy am I glad to see you Niall. It seems ages since you were here.'

He had left in the early hours and was starving. Claire put on a pan of bacon and sausages. Niall went into the bathroom and had a shower while it was cooking.

She knew better than to question the hungry man before he was fed. They ate in silence and Niall went through two pots of tea before he was ready to lean back and relax.

'Oh! That feels better. How have things been here Claire?'

She was disappointed. She had hoped his news would be all about Nessa. She told him about her work with Paddy and her chat with Joe and Mary last night. She told him about Joe being the uncle of a missing person, but that it was a long time ago, twenty-two years.

Niall listened intently. 'The man I am liaising with in Killarney is Detective Inspector Savage, you met him, I believe.'

Claire nodded her head and told him that she had been alarmed to find him here one day after her walk, but that she found him interested in Nessa of course, but the other cases too, which seemed to him similar.

'They are connected Claire. He has convinced me of that. There are a lot of similarities, all women, no further sightings, no evidence of them whatsoever.'

'What does Aidan Savage think might have happened to them Niall?'

Niall hunched his shoulders and stared into his teacup. 'He believes that they are all dead, the ones who didn't leave the country, that is.'

Nessa was shocked to hear this stark answer.

'But he can't be sure of that, can he? There must be an explanation and they possibly are not connected at all. I don't care for his similarities, they are nothing.'

'There has been an investigation going on for years, Claire and the man is convinced that the perpetrator is one person only, probably a psychopath.'

There was such an air of despondency about Niall that chilled Claire.

'We must still keep searching; it could be that Nessa's case is different. We can't just give up, Niall.'

He nodded. 'I don't know what to tell my family. They won't accept if of course. Nessa was always doing daft things and they are certain she is somewhere remote where she cannot contact anyone.'

'What about the islands around? Have the guards been in touch with all of them?'

He nodded sadly. 'None of the missing women were ever sighted on any of them. These are small communities, and any stranger is immediately noted.'

Claire felt sick and knew how Niall must feel too. He was Nessa's favourite brother, and they had a special bond.

'Now Claire, we have to brace ourselves for the television broadcast. I know it's going to be hard, but we have to be brave and remember, we are doing it for Nessa.'

'Will it be held here in the village?'

'Yes, in the school hall as they think it will be the best place. The place will be swarming with journalists afterwards and the morbidly curious. You better be ready for them Claire. They want to show the village and place where Nessa disappeared. We might learn a great deal from this, you know. People remember things that they have sometimes thought of as not important. Any bit of news can throw a new light on the case.'

'Do the police really get a lot of information after a televised appeal?'

'The phones will be hopping Claire, but all too often they are false leads. They all must be taken seriously however, and all information has got to be sifted through. It demands a lot of manpower, which is always scarce, God knows.'

'Will I have to say anything, Niall?'

'I don't know, Aidan Savage will let us know how to proceed. He has lots of experience. I know that he is not keen on emotional outbursts, so I hope I can hold myself together if I have to speak about Nessa.'

He looked so downcast. Claire reached out and took his hand. 'We'll get through this, Niall. We have to do it for Nessa.'

The television crew arrived after lunch and set up their equipment in the school hall.

Aidan Savage arrived at four o'clock with some other officers. Niall drove to the village to liaise with them and discuss how the appeal would be managed and two guards from outlying villages also appeared and went around the village explaining what was happening and urging people to watch their televisions that night and try to help find the missing girl.

The newspaper people also appeared and before dark, had gone around photographing the picturesque village and interviewing the people living there.

Most of the people they spoke to were unaware that anyone was missing and thought the appeal was for Elizabeth Cooney, who went missing a long time ago. This too interested the newspaper people and before long they were asking if there were a serial killer loose in this part of the country.

Detective Savage met with them and asked them to act responsibly and to try and understand the feelings of the villagers. There had never been any whiff of scandal in this village so they should not be stirring things up and confusing people with a case that happened more than twenty-two years ago.

This was what worried the man. He knew the media could play havoc in a community; gossip and imaginings would abound, and people would be confused. How would that help his investigation?

He sighed and was thankful that they had a good couple of weeks of quiet investigation done already. Some information now could be very helpful, he thought.

He felt sorry for the brother of Nessa. Would he be able to stand up under pressure; especially from the media, which was often capable of suggesting all sorts of things? Perhaps the redhaired friend would be a better bet. He was going to talk to the people in the shop and post office and ask if they would attend the meeting in the school hall. After the television crew had done their job, people were inclined to come and chat, and something might be learned then.

Joe and Mary decided to close the shop early and attend the meeting at the school hall. Joe was interested in meeting with this detective and sounding him out about his niece's disappearance.

At seven o'clock the hall was busy with engineers testing the audio equipment and the locals were coming in and slowly filling up the chairs that were available. The media people had to make do with what they could find. Some of the experienced ones sat on the floor in the front.

Detective Savage warned them about using flash photography.

Claire and Niall were extremely nervous. Aidan Savage spoke sternly to them and that calmed them down. He told them that finding Nessa was up to their performance and calmness in talking about her. They must remember that someone out there might have vital information and to focus on reaching that person. They must not let their feelings distract them, 'keep calm at all times and keep a clear head'.

Niall and Claire took their places at the table. They were not prepared for the bright lights and were at first startled. Then it was time to read the carefully prepared speeches that the detective had taken a long time to compose with them and helped them write. The words all looked blurred, and Claire's heart was beating fast and loudly, she thought. She prayed to be able to concentrate on the words and to try to forget the audience.

Claire looked down at the packed hall and felt her heart constrict with fright. Beside her, she could feel Niall start to tremble and reached for his hand to reassure him.

Savage was interested to hear the facts from Joe and asked numerous questions.

Joe was looking flushed but happy. 'I was listened to for the first time. I think they are investigating it, even if it was years ago.'

Niall nodded his head.

'All these cases are now being examined in detail and it's surprising how information comes to light, even years afterwards. Some people keep secrets to spare their families, even when they suspect wrongdoing. If they thought they could prevent these things happening again, they would surely have come forward sooner.'

They all agreed. Niall thought they needed a good night's rest after the excitement and nervous energy expended. Claire agreed.

'You alright driving after that whiskey, girl?' he asked.

'I am Niall. It was what I needed but now I need my bed. What will happen tomorrow do you think?'

'It depends on the response. Aidan is staying locally for a few days to see what happens. He'll be at the station in Knocknabó and I'll join them there tomorrow.'

'Oh, wouldn't it be wonderful if some calls come through? It's hard to believe that anything will really happen, isn't it?' Claire was scepical.

Niall cautioned them not to get their hopes up; things happen slowly, he warned.

'It's like doing a jigsaw,' he muttered as he went out the door.

He drove behind Claire and noticed the number of cars still outside the school hall. Hopefully, the numbers put on the television screen were being used.

The guards in the school hall were on duty until one in the morning in the chance of calls coming in late.

Detective Savage sat and told the guards about the conversation he had with Joe Cooney. A couple of younger guards had not associated the disappearance of the eighteen-year-old with the nearby village.

There was a map spread on the big table and red circles showed the areas where most of the women had disappeared.

A flurry of phone calls interrupted their chat and opinions. Afterwards, they relayed the latest information. Two of the phone calls had come from Cork and Dublin. The information was that two of the 'missing' women had left intentionally and did not want their families to know of their whereabouts.

All information was treated confidentially. It was explained that they would be approached by a plainclothes guard in the coming week just to confirm that the call was genuine, the fear being that someone might try to divert attention away from a genuinely missing person. Both callers understood

112

and even offered to present themselves at a police station.

The map was consulted again and the list of missing women. The two names were found but had not been in this area but much further away in the midlands.

At one o'clock, one guard was left to stay and would be relieved at seven the next morning. It happened that sometimes a call would come through in the early hours, possible because it was a quieter time to ring, and households would be generally asleep. Sometimes too, a night worker on a late shift would make an anonymous call and there were plenty of them. They had to be investigated, of course, and it was often a wild goose chase which upset the investigating officers, wasted time when the real culprit was still getting away with murder.

The lone guard ate his late supper and boiled some water in the kitchen for tea. He did not think that anyone else would ring. It was November and he believed that most people with anything to say would wait until it was daylight.

The phone rang about four o'clock and he was immediately alert. It was a young sounding female voice. She was obviously nervous, and he tried to put her at her ease and get her to slow down.

The story came out in bits and pieces. Firstly, she was anxious that her parents would not hear of it. She had told her parents that she was going to the cinema with her friend. This was not true; both the young ladies had decided to go to a club in the town. They had a good time and had a couple of drinks. Then they had to leave as both their parents expected them in by twelve at the latest. They had to hitch a lift back and her friend was dropped off first. When it was her turn to be dropped the man did not want to drop her off and drove her to a lonely spot, further down the road. She did not know what to do. As soon as he slowed down and pulled into a wooded area, she opened the door and ran for her life. She was on the main road again and a few houses were now in view. She sneaked a look over her shoulder and there was no car following her. At last she could see her own house, and composed herself to enter as quietly as possible. Lucky for her, her parents were in bed and just called out to her as she passed their room. She could not tell them what had happened but discussed it with her friend the next day.

The guard asked her when it had happened.

'Saturday night, the day after Halloween, please do not tell my parents. They will never allow me to go out again if they find out. I'm only just sixteen. Do you really have to know my name?'

He told her that her misadventure could have ended in rape or murder; by making a statement to the police she could prevent it happening again and she might help save a life. He urged her to come in

114

and make that statement. She told him she would have to speak with her friend and if she were willing, they would both come in, so long as it was kept confidential.

She seemed happier when assured of that.

It ended with the girl promising to try and remember anything she could about the car and a description of the man.

The guard made meticulous notes of the phone call and knew that it was a genuine call. He hoped that it was on his duty that a breakthrough might occur.

There were no more calls that night. At seven o'clock the next shift started, and the detectives were informed about the information received and were all present within the hour to hear the latest report about the early morning call.

Chapter 18

Claire woke late and felt drained and weary. She knew then that she needed a trip home to see her parents and family. Niall had already left it seemed. She showered and felt a bit better.

After a cup of tea, she drove again into the village. There were several cars outside the school hall, and she parked nearby and went to see if she could see Niall and tell him about her plans to go home.

There were six men huddled around a map on the big table. She shyly approached waiting for Niall to be free.

Aidan spotted her and beckoned her over.

'We have already had several calls Claire, you will be glad to hear. Scraps of information, forgotten things that somehow came to mind. All in all, it's a positive response and we'll be here all day analysing and making extensive notes and of course, there may be more calls.'

Niall looked around and nodded to the girl, 'yes, it is quite promising Claire. I am thrilled.'

She was dumbfounded. There had been a response! Would any of the calls lead to Nessa?

She sat down as the men chatted and reviewed the situation. She was cautiously optimistic now and the idea of going home suddenly evaporated. She felt the need to go and have a coffee with Mary in the shop. But first she would ring her family and reassure them, again.

'What about this abduction? It's just a couple of miles from here, and only days ago?' Niall was desperate for what they knew. 'Surely he would not dare strike so soon after the supposed abduction of Nessa?'

Aidan shook his head. 'We hope to meet the young girl and get her statement.'

Niall gave a heartfelt sigh. 'I have a feeling that it will be a wild goose chase, this one. Why would he attempt to pick up two girls, isn't that risky?'

'It may be that when one was dropped off that he saw an opportunity and decided to take it. After all, it was late, and poor weather conditions. He must have felt that he was unknown to them, therefore he was not a local.' Aidan stood up and stretched his arms over his head.

'Also, it was very soon after Nessa was abducted, as you say. It might be totally unrelated to the long-time missing women.' Aidan was vocalising whatever thoughts seemed logical to him.

Niall agreed with him. 'That's what we're up against, that's why investigations take so long.'

Claire found both Joe and Mary in the shop. There were customers coming and going and Claire knew it would be difficult to talk just then. Mary saw her however and after finishing with her customer, she beckoned Claire to come with her.

They went into the house and Mary put on the kettle. She wanted to hear if there had been any response and was amazed when Claire told her there had been some phone calls. She could not say anything more as she knew nothing about the calls and they were confidential, she told Mary.

'Everyone in the village has been in and talking about nothing else today. I suppose it's the same in every village and town here. It has affected the whole province these past years. People are inclined to forget though and this appeal on television was a great way of getting people to talk about the women again.'

Mary poured the tea and couldn't stop talking about the excitement in the village. 'I feel most sorry for Agnes, Elizabeth's mother. She thinks her daughter has been forgotten about all this time. Joe does his best to reassure her that she is not forgotten at all and there is still hope in finding out what happened.'

Claire felt that it was Nessa that was forgotten about. All that was talked about, was the missing women of years ago. This happened less than a month ago, for heaven's sake. She said nothing and just listened to Mary.

'Andy wants to bring Paddy down again this afternoon Claire if that's alright.' She looked across at the pale girl opposite her. 'Are you feeling alright, love? You look a bit tired.'

'Yes Mary, I feel a bit battered by it all. Tell Andy it's alright to bring Paddy. A little bit of distraction might help.'

'You should get a bit of fresh air, girl, that's what you need now. Go for a walk on the beach, why don't you?'

Yes, Claire thought. That might be what I need to blow away the fuzziness in my brain and clear my mind.

When Claire left the shop to walk to her car, she was met by a few women who stopped to talk to her. She was now well known around the place and after the appeal, they all understood the girl's anxiety about her friend.

They all assured her that they were praying that Nessa would be found. All doubted that anyone in their village was responsible.

One woman, walking alone, crossed the road to speak to her as she neared her car. She confided that she had nearly been abducted one night coming home from Knocknabó. Only that someone had slowed down at that moment and scared whoever it was, it could have been her.

Claire asked her if she had notified the guards?

'Oh, it was years ago, they would hardly be interested in me now, would they?'

'Of course! They would be extremely interested. This investigation is about all the women in the area and beyond who went missing. You could contribute something very valuable. You must contact them. Better still, drop into the school hall now and ask for Detective Savage.'

The woman was still unconvinced. 'But sure, here I am. *I'm* not missing, am I?'

'That's not the point, you could well have been another victim, don't you see?'

The woman was still doubtful looking, and Claire was getting exasperated.

'Look, come with me. I will bring you there and you will have nothing to fear. A few words are just what they want.'

The woman was so nervous, and Claire began to wonder if she was making the story up. She took the woman's arm and walked determinedly towards the hall.

'What's your name, by the way?' she wanted to keep the woman distracted until they were inside.

'Anne Murphy. I'm not sure if this is a good idea. My husband might be cross with me. I never told him about it. I hadn't met him then.'

They entered the hall and Claire marched Anne across the room to where Aidan and Niall were sitting hunched over a computer.

Briefly Claire explained that Anne had something to tell them. Aidan offered the woman a chair and suggested that Claire stay also.

It was all recalled again, and Anne answered all the questions put to her. She did not seem nervous now, having been told that her story might help in the finding of the perpetrator. Claire listened as the woman answered the usual questions.

Anne had left a relative's house in Knocknabó, where she had been visiting. It was in March and very cold. She had intended to walk the three or four miles home as her bicycle had a puncture and she left it with her relative. As she neared the village a vehicle had stopped, and she was offered a lift. Something in the manner of the man put her off, plus the fact that she did not recognise him. He became insistent when she refused and then left the car and tried to pull her into it. Luckily, another car coming from behind, slowed down and the man jumped back in and sped off.

The other driver asked if everything was alright, and she assured him it was. She had not recognised that driver either and was not the sort to take risks, so did not accept his offer either. She almost ran the rest of the way home.

Niall was taking notes and stopped to commend the woman. 'Lord you are a brave woman! Two offers of a lift in the one night and you refused. The second one might have been innocent, I'd say.'

'Well, I did not know the man, either man, they were not local, so I didn't take the offer.'

'Good for you. In the first case I would say you had a lucky escape Anne.' Aidan looked at the woman.

He had a way of asking questions with his head turned away but looking straight into the eyes of the person. It often disconcerted people and threw them a bit.

'What type of car was he driving Anne?'

She frowned. 'It was a long time ago and it was over in seconds. I think it was old and dark coloured, I seem to remember it being higher than a normal car, maybe a jeep or something of that sort. Mind you, I am hopeless when it comes to cars. I know nothing of makes or anything else. As I say, it lasted seconds and "old and dark and bulky", are the things that stand out now. Even the other fellow's car, I can't remember at all. Hopeless, I am!'

The men thanked Anne and said she was very good to come in and talk to them. They felt her information was solid and that it could be important in this case.

As Claire accompanied Anne out of the room, she turned and thanked Claire for making her come.

'Lord, I feel a whole lot better after getting that out. I never told anyone before. I would like to think that I helped.'

'I know what you mean. Hopefully, they will find my friend, but it's not looking good Anne.'

Chapter 19

The guards waited all afternoon for the call from the girl who had contacted them at four in the morning. By six they were packing up and getting ready to go back to their different stations.

Detective Savage and Niall wanted to stay on for a while longer. Niall brought sandwiches and coffee over at six and the two settled in to wait for another hour or two at the most.

At six thirty the call came. It was the young girl, sounding nervous and wanting to speak to the guard she had spoken to before. Aidan assured her that he had passed on her information and that he had stayed to hear her story.

Again, she reiterated the need for confidentiality, and he reassured her. The other girl, her friend would not talk about it as she had not witnessed what she had, plus the fact, that they had a couple of drinks.

Aidan was a persuasive listener, calm, unhurried and not overtalkative. He leaned back and switched on the recorder having explained that he would do this to later digest everything she had said.

The girls had left the club at the early time of eleven forty-five. Their parents were very strict. A car had stopped, and they had supposed it was someone who had been at the club. It was raining by now and they had not wanted to get wet. They sat in the back and had a giggling fit. They had not spoken to the driver who had the radio on. The girls finished what was left in the half bottle of vodka there and then and put the empty bottle down the side of the seat. When her friend saw her estate approaching, she called out for the driver to drop her here. She asked if he would go a bit further along and let her friend out at the cottages.

When the girl who remained asked him to stop, he said he would just go up further to turn around as he was not going in this direction. She accepted this, until he pulled into the wooded area that was known as a courting spot for couples. He had leaned over the seat and grinned in at her in the back seat. Then she knew she was in trouble and jumped out of the car and ran as fast as she could down the laneway and onto the main road, where there was traffic passing. She knew she was safe then, as her house came into view. Looking behind she saw that there was no car coming after her.

That was all, she said, and there was nothing more.

'Well done, young lady. That was a most articulate report, and we are very grateful to you. However, we do need to ask a few questions, as you will understand.'

'But I have told you everything, honest.'

'We believe you too. But we need to try and get you to remember details while they are still fresh in your memory, alright? Now, what do you remember about the man, did you see his face?'

'Well not really. It was dark, as I said, we were in the back seat.'

'What about his hair, what colour was it and did you see any distinguishing features at all?'

'We couldn't see his hair at all, he had a woollie cap pulled right down over his ears. It was cold and wet, you know?'

'Alright. Did you notice if he spoke with an accent?'

'He didn't really speak, he kinda grunted when we asked him to stop at Lisa's house. He only mumbled about going further down the road, it was hardly audible, but I grasped what he meant.'

'Right, now the car, what do you remember about that?'

'Well it was not a flash car, I assure you. That's what set us off giggling. It was an old banger; a biggish lump of a thing, dark, maybe black, I dunno, really. I nearly fell when I jumped out, it was higher than a normal car, you know?'

They had got all that there was to get, and it was recorded. They again thanked the girl and told her if she or her friend remembered anything later or even weeks later, not to hesitate to contact them. They would type up the recorded interview and would she come and sign it whenever she could? Aidan also told her that she was a lucky girl and never to hitch a lift again, it was not worth it.

'I know. We've promised each other that we'll never risk it again. 'I'll call into Knocknabó station next week if that's alright.'

When they locked up the school hall, Aidan wondered how the young girls now could be so dumb, with all their so-called sophistication.

'Honestly, barely sixteen, out without their parents' knowledge, drinking vodka and accepting lifts from strangers, it's a disaster waiting to happen, Niall.'

'And you have daughters, Aidan! The teen years must age a parent, I think. It's strange isn't it, two attempted abductions, years apart. What chances are they being the same person, do you think?'

'They all described similar vehicles although that would be unusual; someone having the same jalopy over what? Ten years? How long ago did Anne say her encounter happened?'

Niall opened his book. 'Yep, almost ten years ago.'

The men walked to their cars. Aidan would return to Killarney tonight. There would be a conference there in a couple of days and all the recent information would be collated and people set to check facts.

Niall would join him there at the conference. He hoped to get a good rest before that and wanted to ring his parents now and give them all the latest. They had all watched the appeal on television and he hoped they were bearing up under the enormous strain.

When he finally got to the cottage it was after eight. There was a welcome meal. On his arrival Claire put a steak under the grill for him. She had eaten at seven when Andy brought Paddy back home.

She recounted her time with Paddy and said that the boy was more relaxed and calmer than he had been at first. He was learning the letters of the alphabet but was better with numbers. His drawing was good, and it was another way of communicating for him.

He took up a copy book and looked through it as he ate his dinner.

'He certainly likes ladies with red hair, I'm thinking.' He laughed when he saw her blush.

'He also likes cars, just look at all those drawings,' she said.

'Yep, what a pity his mother did not seek help for him earlier.'

Claire asked him if any more calls had come through. He said there were interesting developments.

She reminded him about Anne. Niall and Aidan were so grateful for her bringing the woman over.

'Ever thought of joining the guards, Claire?'

She shook her head and said her chosen job satisfied her.

He told her that he would be off to Killarney the day after tomorrow and that all the latest information would be sifted.

As he sat by the fire with a glass of wine, he mused about the attempted abductions. 'Yes, there was another one, but I can't say anything about that.'

They discussed how strange that it should happen in the same area, and near enough to the area where Elizabeth had disappeared.

'It's not as if it's on the motorway or near it. It is really off the beaten track wouldn't you say, Niall?'

'It is a fairly rural area, and that guy must pass it regularly I would think, if the cases are connected. That means we must examine the whole part of the country where it has happened. Not that it makes the guy local, but it's familiar territory for him, I think. He could have grown up around here.'

'It was also late at night in both cases you mentioned and that's important too I think,' said Claire. 'You need to be familiar with these roads, especially in the dark.'

Niall nodded. 'Gosh I don't think I can take much more of this living without television and phone and all that. Not being able to ring someone or even just browse is alien to me now. It might have been alright for Nessa, but I don't have the artistic temperament. What about you Claire?'

'I am reaching the end of my tolerance too, I think. I need to be able to at least reach people. I miss the news on telly too. I never thought I would say that.'

'Right, I'm off Claire. I must be up early and go and see the lads in Knocknabó. I might go and see Elizabeth Cooney's mother too just in case she can remember something new after all this time.'

He turned before entering the bedroom. 'I wonder whether you would feel up to coming with me; I think women respond better when there is a female present; it takes the pressure off a bit.' He looked at her quizzically.

'I certainly would like to come if I won't be in the way. I might think of some questions that you don't. What do you think? Can I ask questions too Niall, or would that be inappropriate?'

Niall laughed. 'Not at all Claire, you can ask away, it will all help. It's just an informal chat that I want.'

Chapter 20

Claire was low on food again. The fridge freezer was small and did not hold much. She needed to go to town and get fresh meat. Niall said they should see Mrs. Cooney first as she always attended morning Mass and would be up and about anyway. Joe had arranged a meeting with her, and she was excited to be interviewed after all this time. She had a great fear of dying without knowing what had happened to her girl.

She invited her best friend Nora to come in and help allay her nerves. Nora was also her daughter's godmother.

They were shown into the sitting room and Niall and Claire tried their best to put the woman at her ease. They had been warned by Joe that she suffered from her nerves.

'What a lovely Christmas Cactus, it's blooming early, isn't it? Claire admired the beautiful house plant. It was spectacular.

Agnes was pleased and told Claire how she had grown it from a leave from one of her friend's plants.

'Really? Is it that easy to grow them, Agnes?'

This chatter helped to divert attention away from the real purpose of the visit. Niall was relieved as he could see the woman relaxing already. Nora also made a few useful remarks on the growing of house plants.

Then Nora asked them if they would like tea. Niall immediately said no, and Claire said yes, both simultaneously.

Everyone laughed and Nora said she would make a pot and went off into the kitchen.

Niall began by asking about Elizabeth and where she had grown up; schools she had attended.

Agnes started to get nervous again and rubbed her forehead. 'I can never remember dates and things; I forget a lot these days.'

Claire spoke then and said soothingly, 'Agnes, it doesn't matter a bit about dates, just talk about her and what she was like; what sort of girl she was and things she was interested in, you know?'

'Oh, that'll be easy. She was always a noisy, boisterous sort of child, I have to say. There was never a quiet day in this house with her around. That's why it was so awful when she went.' The woman paused and gazed into the distance.

Niall went to ask a question, but Claire elbowed him, as he was sitting beside her on the sofa.

The silence only lasted a minute and then Agnes sighed and went on with the story.

'She was as bright as a button at school and was always top of the class. Mind you, she could be a right little show-off too! She loved an audience, but I suppose that's the way with all only children. I would have loved more, but none came. She was our pride and joy, and her father had her spoiled, so he did. Of

131

course, I was the one who tried to discipline her, her father could deny her nothing.' She smiled at her memories.

Nora poured the tea and handed it around. Niall was glad of Claire's presence, he would never have thought that Agnes would be so forthcoming and knew that if it were up to him, the woman would have dried up ages ago.

Nora added to the conversation now and noted various events in Elizabeth's life; her confirmation, her athletic ability and the medals she had won for Irish dancing. She was an all-rounder Nora said, and Agnes nodded her head and dabbed her eyes.

'She was so stylish you know. She could have been a model; she certainly had the self-confidence for it.' Nora nodded and nibbled at her biscuit while Agnes again nodded.

Now Niall decided it was time to make his presence felt. 'Did Elizabeth have many friends, Agnes?'

'Many friends? Sure everyone wanted to be friends with her, she had loads of friends, even people she didn't go to school with. She was so popular you wouldn't believe.'

'Did she have a boyfriend, Agnes?' he asked gently.

'Oh no! Sure she had only completed her Leaving Certificate and was planning the party for it with the rest of the class. No, we would not have liked her having boyfriends at that age. It's a long time ago and I know the young people are different now and behave differently but it was not so lax then, believe me. We always told her, "there's time enough for boyfriends later".'

Niall thought about the 'barely' sixteen-year-old from the nearby village who had escaped serious assault or rape or worse just the weekend before and had to wonder if life changed so drastically in twenty odd years.

They chatted a while about modern life and what life was like for Elizabeth.

'Well, you know, we were not flush with money, so she had to earn her pocket money and she did. She helped out Joe in the shop when she could, and she also babysat for people around and helped to keep an eye on young Paddy up the mountain. He was a handful for his mother, you know. A bit backward, as we say, and she minded him a lot and brought him for walks and generally helped out there.'

'What had she been hoping to do with her life?'

Claire was wondering what such a gifted girl could hope to do in a village as small as this.

Agnes smiled sadly, 'she wanted to work with children and was talking about nursing or perhaps teaching. She had not made up her mind.'

They could see that Agnes was tiring and Niall decided to bring the interview to an end.

'Agnes and Nora, it was lovely talking to you both and you have painted a lovely picture of Elizabeth. I hope we can tie up all these cases of missing women soon and that you will get some answers. You certainly deserve them and to know what happened her. Agnes, you know after all this time that the outcome will probably be sad, don't you?'

The woman nodded slowly, and tears ran down her face. 'I know, she is with her father now and I get my consolation in that knowledge.'

The two rose from the sofa and Claire went over and sat beside Agnes and put her arms around the woman. She held her for a moment and then kissed her cheek.

As they went out to the car, Nora followed. She took Claire's arm and pulled her to one side.

Claire looked at her with the question in her eyes.

'Nora looked behind her and then quietly said, 'Listen, I know her mother thinks she was a saint, and I am not saying she was a bad girl, do you get me? All I'm saying is, Betty was not *that* innocent, and she did have a boyfriend but who he was, I have no idea, I just know she had a man in her life. Women sense these things.'

Claire nodded, 'I know what you mean; women *do* sense these things. Thanks for that, and we'll keep it under our hats, okay?'

Nora patted her arm. 'I knew you would understand. I wouldn't have told his nibs there.'

On the way to the town, Claire relayed what Nora had said and they discussed the interview and what they learned. Niall looked at Claire as they parked outside the supermarket in town. 'I would never have learned as much by myself, Claire, we make a great team. Have you really *neve*r considered becoming a Garda?'

Claire chuckled. 'You do have quite an interesting job and I would love this aspect of it; trying to solve mysteries and crime. I would love to be able to give people like Agnes the answers to the questions which surely stay with them every day of their lives.'

Niall nodded and agreed with her. He knew though, that answers were not always found and that the parents of missing people would usually live out their lives not knowing the answers.

Chapter 21

They went to the town and got some groceries which Niall insisted on paying for, as he told Claire that she had been buying food since she came.

The daily newspapers had stories about the television appeal in Kilshee and the media had managed to resurrect a few blurred photographs of missing women and there was a fresh photo of Nessa heading one of the articles. Niall had supplied that, but Claire could not bear to look at the paper.

They returned shortly to the cottage and after a sandwich lunch, Niall left to join his colleagues in Knocknabó. Claire sat and went over Nora's whispered information about Joe's niece. Would any of her friends from back then know about the boyfriend. She realised that they should have got a list of friends from school or best friends. She wondered if she would be considered nosy if she paid another quick visit to Agnes. Certainly not today, the poor woman had been through an ordeal this morning. Maybe tomorrow she would pass by.

At four it was dark, and she had the fire lighting when Andy and Paddy presented themselves as usual. Today Paddy offered her a bag of various chocolate bars. He smiled shyly when she thanked him. She was pleased and touched with the present, then realised that he would not have thought of that himself, it was probably Andy's idea.

'Don't tell me you walked down in this dark and damp weather Andy.'

'No, we didn't. Margie lent me her car, so we travelled in style, didn't we Paddy?'

'Mam's cah, Ce'h,' repeated Paddy.

'I didn't know you really drove, Andy.'

'Sure, every country boy drives, Claire, I've been driving tractors since I was twelve.'

'What about a licence?'

'I have a full licence. Most of the time the driving is on the farm anyway. Dad is fussy though and made me do my test and it proved handy when I was in New Zealand.'

'You must miss it, Andy, do you?'

Andy nodded and turning to Claire said, 'We better get on with this lesson. He is excited and wants to show you his 'homework'.'

Paddy was already sitting at the table and now he opened the plastic file that she had provided him with the last time, to hold his copy books, drawings and colouring pencils.

He showed her all his drawings and had written under them in his own strange writing, what they were.

Claire appreciated the time and effort that had gone into them and praised him. She took one of the papers up and looked intently at it. There was that rectangular item again, this time coloured pink, all the little buttons had numbers on them, even if they were hard to see. She knew immediately what it was.

'Lovely, Paddy. That's a mobile phone, isn't it?'

The boy/man was pleased with the recognition and beamed at them both. Andy took it and looked closely at the drawing.

'Janey, it's fantastic, so it is. Paddy you are a genius.'

Paddy nodded and a string of his language followed. Then he pointed to his latest car. It too was very well executed and even had number plates on it, a sting of tiny numbers and letters.

Claire and Andy were amazed at the detail in the drawings. Paddy was not so simple at all, but he was certainly an enigma. He obviously understood a lot of what went on around him. How frustrating it must be for him not to be able to communicate his thoughts.

Claire continued with the cardboard letters of the alphabet she had cut out. Paddy was really more interested in drawing, but between herself and Andy, they coaxed him to look up and sound out the various letters. They even played a game where Andy would say the wrong sound for a letter and then Paddy would correct him. It was a lot of fun and the three enjoyed it.

They were all laughing loudly, when the door opened, and Niall entered. Claire could not believe that it was after six already.

Paddy was introduced to Niall and shook his hand shyly. 'Hello Paddy, I'm Niall.'

Paddy immediately said, 'Mm Pah.'

'How is the sheep farming going, Andy?'

Andy scowled and shook his head. 'We've had a few losses with bloody dogs. It's heart breaking so it is, to see those poor animals ripped apart and most of them in lamb too.'

Niall commented that the owner had the legal right to shoot any dog found roaming free.

Andy agreed and said that Mick was now coming to the end of his tether. Every night he patrolled the fields. There were posters up warning people to keep their dogs in at night and use a leash when walking them on the common land and woods.

'What is wrong with people?' asked Claire. 'Don't they know the damage these dogs can do?'

Niall agreed and said that the owners should be prosecuted made to pay the value of the animals.

'The owners should be made to come and see the damage their darling dogs have done,' Claire said.

'Come on Paddy, your Ma will have your supper ready. Will we see you tomorrow Claire, maybe for a shorter lesson? You are doing great with him.'

'We never even had time for tea lads, so tomorrow we must have tea with those chocolate bars Paddy.

Chapter 22

'Is there any more news, Niall, any sighting of Nessa at all?' Claire was feeling strange and disoriented again. There was too much going on in some ways and nothing at all in other ways. She felt she was in danger of forgetting her friend at times.

'No credible sightings of her, at all, Claire. There were three sightings, one in Madrid, one in the Titanic Museum in Belfast and one in Dublin. They are being investigated of course. The emphasis is now on the other women who went missing, in the hope that it will throw some light on Nessa.'

'I just feel all of you have given up hope, I don't hear her name mentioned anymore, it's upsetting me.'

'Do you not think that I am upset too? My parents are now worried stiff, they finally accept that something has happened their only daughter. The other brothers want to come and descend on the village and start their own search. Aidan doesn't want it as it might make the person responsible, disappear, move away or just go to ground.'

Claire could see that the man before her was worried and she felt guilty for bringing her worries to the fore. Nessa's family would all be concerned, of course, and they must think that nothing was being done either.

'Her booking and car were confirmed as arriving on the date and no return booking was confirmed or sight of her car which is now registered as missing. It must be somewhere; a car doesn't just disappear either. There is a lot of work going on behind the scenes Nessa, it's just not obvious to the members of the public.'

'Sorry for being a pain, Niall. I feel so helpless. What about that missed call from her phone, that is something that I keep thinking about.'

'There is someone working on that and checking all satellite signals in surrounding areas. Difficult enough given the restricted coverage. I'm not giving up hope on that.'

They ate their meal in silence, each busy with their own thoughts. Both were trying to remain optimistic but as the days went by with no communication with Nessa, their hopes were slowly fading.

The next morning Niall was off to Killarney to meet the team working together on the missing women case. He would not be back that night probably, he told Claire and again warned her to be in before dark.

Claire made her way to Knocknabó after ten and met with Agnes as she arrived home from Mass. She was surprised to see Claire again. She welcomed her with a smile and invited her in.

'You're on your own today, I see. I thought the police always worked in twos.'

'I'm no policewoman, Agnes. I teach children with special needs. I am a good friend of Nessa, Niall's brother, whom you met yesterday.'

They sat in the small sitting room and Agnes lit the gas fire.

'You poor girl, I saw the telly the other night and it was only then it dawned on me, that this nightmare is still going on.'

'Yours started a long time ago Agnes, Elizabeth must have been the first in this area.'

'I wouldn't say that love, before Elizabeth went, there were a couple of girls went away, but people then usually believed the girls had gone to England for one reason or another.'

'Why would they not keep in touch with family?'

'Oh, I don't know that. Sometimes in big families there are fallings out about different things.'

'Can I make you a cup of tea Claire?'

'Not at all Agnes, let me make you one.'

'Alright love, me legs are not the best now. You'll find everything in the kitchen.'

When Claire brought in the tray with the tea, she found Agnes looking through a photo album.

'That's what I really came to talk to you about Agnes. Do you have a photo I could take with me, also a list of friends of hers, people she was friendly with and spent time with?'

'The photo is the easy part Claire. Most of her friends are long gone from here. There are some in Dublin and one in Killarney I think.'

The woman took out a photo from the album. 'This is Liz on her first Communion day. There are lots here of her on different occasions.'

Claire looked at the photos of the beautiful girl with the abundance of red hair, like her own. She could see at a glance that Elizabeth was a sophisticated looking teenager. In some photos she would pass as a lot older. Her dress was typical of the nineties, very short skirts and cropped tops. She calculated and realised that Elizabeth would now be forty if she had lived.

'Red hair seems to run in your family I see.'

'Not in mine, but on the Cooney side definitely. Look at Andy.'

Claire laughed. 'Yes, he and I could be related, he told me, when we first met.'

'Is there anyone in the village here or nearby who was friendly with Elizabeth?'

'Let me see now.' Agnes closed her eyes and went through all the girls who were in the same class as her daughter twenty-two years ago.

'The only one still here in the village is Nora's daughter. You met her yesterday. She was Elizabeth's godmother, and I was godmother to her daughter Maria.'

'Is she married here?'

'Yes, to a lovely fellow. He owns the hardware store on the main street. She has two children and often helps in the shop. Nora has been a great help to her, collecting the children from school and that. You might talk with her. She might know of more people. My mind is bad these days. The troubles of that time unhinged me a bit, that and Andrew dying.'

'It must have been an awful time for you Agnes. I don't know how anyone could cope with that. I'm finding it hard now and so is Niall and the family.'

'Yes, it's something you never get used to.' Agnes dabbed her eyes with a tissue.

'Did Elizabeth have many hobbies?'

'She was very into these musical gigs and loved the music groups and all that. We were strict with her but now and again she was allowed to attend a concert, if we knew who was going with her. Apart from that she collected postcards and different arty stuff from all over.'

She pointed her finger at a box up on a shelf above the television. 'Claire, if you get that box down, I will show you a few of her precious items.'

Claire obliged and Agnes opened the tin biscuit box and took out a handful of cards and letters. She looked quickly through the cards and opened a few of the cards. There were little snippets of poetry in some of them and Claire smiled.

'I also like poetry Agnes and so does Nessa. It looks like Elizabeth did too.'

'Why don't you take them and look at them at your leisure Claire? I'm afraid I'm rather tired now, love.'

'Oh Agnes! I do apologise. I did not mean to stay so long. Can I do anything for you before going?'

'Not a thing. My dinner will be delivered shortly and then I'll have a nap. I don't sleep too good most nights.'

'I will bring all these things back to you soon Agnes and thank you so much for your time.'

'It was no hardship, I just love talking about her, Claire. It's all I have now, memories and most people don't like bringing her name up at all.'

Claire kissed Agnes again and promised to be back soon.

Chapter 23

Claire drove down the main street and looked for the hardware shop. There it was on the corner, opposite the post office. She sat outside and wondered if she should chance intruding again. She thought of Nessa and that decided her.

Entering the hardware shop, she saw a handsome man serving a customer and looked around for a woman. There was a woman in the office, could that be his wife? She looked about forty.

Timidly she knocked on the office door. The woman looked up and saw her and rose to go out to her. Claire felt awkward introducing herself and explaining her mission.

'I saw you on television the other night; everyone here would recognise you now.' She gave a small smile.

Claire explained that she had been to see Agnes and wondered if she could tell her anything about Elizabeth Cooney.

The woman looked startled. 'Elizabeth? That was years ago! Is she connected to the present girl's disappearance?'

Claire hastened to tell her that the investigation into all missing women was ongoing and there might be a connection or might not.

'Well come in and take a seat. I'll tell you all I know about Lizzie.'

The office was warm, and Claire was glad to sit down. The shop was busy with lots of coming and going and Maria was interrupted often to give change or take orders.

What sort of childhood did they have here and what could Maria tell her about the sort of girl she was and who her friends were?

'We had the usual happy childhood really. Nothing out of the ordinary. We all attended the same school in the village and played camogie and learned Irish dancing. Lizzie excelled in everything and was popular. She was a pleasant child and interested in everything. She loved small children and by the age of ten, used to be asked to babysit for the women with small babies. She loved that job and got paid for it too.'

Claire nodded. 'Yes, I heard from Mary in the shop in Kilshee that she used to mind Paddy, up the mountain, who was a bit slow.'

'Yes, she was very patient with him and said that he was a challenge to her. She was one to love a challenge; anything that came too easy, she soon tired of.'

Claire told Maria that her mother had already told her that she suspected that the missing girl had a boyfriend that the parents knew nothing about. What did Maria know?

'Oh of course she had boyfriends. She started at fourteen, she was much more grownup and sophisticated that the rest of us. We were all mad jealous.'

In between the interruptions, Claire got a picture of a spirited and lively girl, one who knew she was a magnet for men and learned early how to take advantage of that.

By the time she was sixteen she was bored with the boys in the village of similar age. She was not interested in them; she was too advanced and felt she had outgrown the lads there.

Maria knew about all the fellows she had been interested in earlier but became aware that her friend was changing and did not confide as much in her as before. It was around this time that Maria suspected that she had an older boyfriend but surprisingly, Lizzie did not talk about him. Maria and her friends used to wonder who it could be. They still all went out together to the cinema and music gigs, but often Lizzie would cancel at the last minute without any good excuse, they felt.

During the last summer they spent together, Lizzie changed somewhat again. She seemed to become more aggressive and questioned everything. She told the girls that she had no intention of settling down and getting married here. She felt there was a whole big world out there and even thought that Dublin was too small. No, she had designs of starting off in London and then perhaps, the States when she qualified as a children's nurse, or teacher, whatever

148

she decided to do. Most of the girls would be happy to settle down eventually and marry, but Lizzie even told them that they were stupid.

"Think about what a narrow and mean existence you would have here! I want to be able to buy the clothes I like, try different restaurants, go on foreign holidays and live an interesting life. Think any man here could give you that, girls?"

Maria laughed as she recalled the conversation, then was interrupted again, to take money and hand out receipts.

'That was poor Lizzie, she had such high hopes,' she continued as she sat down again. 'That was why we thought she ran away with someone, but who it was, we could not figure out. There was nobody rich or well off in the area that could provide our girl with the life she wanted.'

'Could he have been a married man, did you ever think?' Claire was becoming interested in this girl who had such an appetite for a glamorous life.

'We thought of that, of course, but again, there was nobody that we knew of, that suddenly left his wife and ran off with her. Of course, there could have been someone from Killarney or one of the bigger towns, but where did she meet him? She was always here in the village. Our lives revolved around here and the nearby villages like Kilshee. She sometimes helped in her uncle Joe's shop there.'

149

Claire asked Maria if she had married a local and learned that she had. She had done a secretarial course and had lived in Dublin for few years but got lonely and came back. Her husband was a villager, one of the many young men who had once been infatuated with Liz.

'Did you resent that Maria, that Lizzie could have such an effect on men?'

'We were grateful for the leftovers,' she laughed. 'Some took it hard naturally when Liz lost interest in them. It was a blow to their male pride. One of the nicer fellows here had a bit of a breakdown after his Leaving Cert and the adults thought it was the strain of all the study. We knew, us girls, that it was the fact that Lizzie had lost interest and moved on to someone else.'

Claire wondered if anyone could have been jealous of her and wished her harm, on account of her fickle behaviour?

'They might have. I don't know. Really there was nobody here that would be her equal. She was intelligent too, though her interest in material things might make her seem shallow. I think she had a good heart under it all.'

'Did anyone leave the village after she went off?'

'Not particularly; by the time the Leaving Cert results came out, a lot of students would leave anyway away; to university or to various places.'

'Who did stay here? Any of the boys that were interested in Lizzie?'

Maria smiled broadly. 'My fellow, Graham. His father had the business, and he had a ready-made career. By the time I returned from Dublin, he had long forgotten the gorgeous Liz and settled for me.'

They both laughed.

'What about the poor boy that had the breakdown? Is he still here, Maria?

'No, he went on for the priesthood a few years later and is now a priest somewhere in the west of Ireland.'

'What did you think of it all Maria?'

Maria sat and pondered that. After a while she told Claire her theory. The fact that Liz became so angry and independent minded, made her think that she had broken up with this older boyfriend. She had seemed so against settling here, that she thought maybe he, being older, had been keen to settle down now and that did not suit Liz. Perhaps she had hoped they would both go off to a different place and begin a life such as the life Liz wanted.

'Maybe his father had a farm or business that he was expected to carry on?' suggested Claire.

'Sounds like my Graham!' Claire laughed and nodded her head. 'Yes, he was expected to stay and carry on the family business alright, but then so were others who were eldest sons on farms and in businesses.'

'Did anyone ever buck the system and take off to live their own choice of life?'

'Oh yes! Plenty of young people did that; some stayed away, but a few returned after a time. What you must realise Claire, is that most of the villages around here are small, and not much changes over the years. It's the bigger towns and cities that have employment opportunities. Even our business is gradually slowing down; it's too difficult to compete with big companies and mass-produced goods. Graham was lucky to inherit this, but it won't be enough for our children. He is hoping to buy a piece of land eventually and go in for organic farming, that sort of thing.'

Claire digested this on the way home and knew that the glamorous Lizzie would not have been content with that sort of life, at least she did not think she would.

Chapter 24

Claire was tired from all the talking and asking questions. She wondered how detectives did the work they did. Surely their heads must ache at the end of the day.

She called to the shop and Mary immediately told her that Andy had been in touch and wondered whether she could go to the farm today as he was driving Margie to Dublin for tests. She had been complaining of her chest for some time. Andy would return home that night and leave Margie at the hospital for the few days needed.

Claire said she would go, and it was not a problem.
She explained that they had seen Agnes the day before and she had again visited the woman this morning. She bought a few items for her supper and then left. She was starving after all the talking and knew she would have to eat immediately.

By four-thirty the cottage kitchen was nice and warm, and Claire was feeling better and more relaxed.

I better not relax too much, or I won't want to go up to Paddy, she thought to herself. She took her big bag and put in the new copy books she had just bought for Paddy. He was certainly getting through them.

It was dark and she drove carefully over the rough track. She could see lights on in the old farmhouse and thought that Mick must be inside and finished his work.

She found Paddy sprawled on the couch in front of the television watching a cartoon programme for kids.

He greeted her with enthusiasm and pulled out his file from the kitchen table drawer at once.

She was touched that the lesson meant so much to him and hoped he was progressing. She did not know for sure and would love to have a professional opinion. She intended to seek some expert advice when she returned to Dublin.

She took out the new copies and his eyes lit up. Then she produced some chocolate bars and he whooped in delight.

They started with the flash cards and he was eager to get the praise that he had come to expect. His sounding was improving. Not for the first time Claire wondered if he had tongue-tie as well as other problems.

Now he was writing numbers and they were excellent except his threes and fives which were, more often than not, the wrong way around, but still recognisable. She did some simple addition, using discs she had found in the shop. He would look at the laid-out discs and write down the number of discs in his copy. He did this without counting them singly as most children would do. Again, she was impressed with this man who was also a child.

She took his copy and wrote a simple sum with a line drawn underneath and wrote in the answer, then wrote in another without the answer. She pointed to the space under the line and asked him how many did the numbers add up to? He laughed at her and wrote the correct number without hesitation.

After several of these exercises she tried subtraction and again after giving him an example with the discs first and then writing an example in the copy book, he again gave the correct answers without any trouble.

She was quite amazed. She had not expected this. She was musing about his intelligence as he again started his drawing, when the kitchen door opened. She looked up, expecting to see Andy. There was a tall and dark-haired man in the doorway.

This must be Mick she surmised and rose to greet the man. He stood still in the doorway staring at her.

'Hello, you must be Mick. I am Claire McKeogh.'

He stepped forward and grasped her hand in his huge hand and smiled. He looked so familiar she was puzzled.

'Hello Claire, so you are the teacher. Indeed, you must be very patient with young Paddy here. Is he behaving himself?'

'He is always a perfect gentleman Mick, and he seems to love his lessons.'

'Would you like a cup of tea Claire? I told Andy and Margie I would be in to give the lad his tea.'

As he moved around the kitchen Claire studied the older man covertly as she supervised Paddy with his drawing. He was in his mid-fifties she guessed and had a striking face. He must have been a stunning looking man in his youth, she thought. There was a sprinkling of grey now in his plentiful black hair. Why was he not married with a family, she wondered?

'Are you related to the Cooneys, Claire? That was the first thing that struck me when I saw you: your hair.'

Claire laughed. 'Andy said the same thing to me on meeting me. No, I have no Cooneys in my family tree. I suppose if we were to go back far enough, we would all be related.'

He laughed and said that was true enough. He took out a casserole from the Aga and ladled out a plate for Paddy and the lad tucked in hungrily.

They chatted amiably as he ate. Claire asked Mick about the sheep as she drank her cup of tea.

He told her the same story about how difficult it was at this time of year with the sheep down from the mountain. They would be bringing them into the big barn after Christmas as the lambing time drew nearer.

'It's a busy life Mick, and hard too. To be out in all this cold weather, day in and day out.'

'You get used to it Claire and it's a healthy life and there is great freedom up here. I love it.'

Claire looked at her watch, 'My goodness, how the time flies when you're busy.'

'Be careful driving in this dark weather Claire. The track can be slippery with all the rain we're getting.'

Claire suddenly remembered that time she had almost collided with him and felt her face flushing.

She hastened to apologise for her careless driving that day. He smiled and told her not to worry about it.

'There was no harm done,' he said as he rose.

'Andy should be back within the hour as they left this morning. He is staying here tonight, as I sometimes have to patrol the fields for those marauding dogs.'

He smiled again, that charming boyish smile and held out his hand. 'Hope we meet again Claire. Margie is very thankful for all the help you have given Paddy.'

He left by the kitchen door.

Claire got up and took the cup over to the sink and Paddy's empty dinner plate. She pulled out a couple of extra chocolate bars and put them beside Paddy.

'That's your reward Paddy for the work well done. You're quite a scholar, now aren't you? We'll have another lesson soon.'

She went and got her coat where she had hung it in the hallway. Going back, Paddy handed her the bag. She told Paddy to go back to his television, he had done enough hard work.

'Ce'h, tanvmun. Pah lyuloh.'

Claire guessed what he was saying and said in reply, 'You are very welcome Paddy and I like you too.'

It was only as she drove slowly along the muddy track that it dawned on her that neither man had spoken to each other at all. Of course, talking would not be possible for Paddy, but he was always a little bit vocal when he was with Andy; and Mick had not spoken directly to Paddy either. Was that the norm in that house, she wondered? Surely they made an attempt to reach the lad. She was sure that Margie would.

She reached the cottage and put more turf on the fire as well as putting on the heating. It was cold and she was so tired. She poured a glass of wine and sat on the sofa going over her busy day.

She certainly had an interesting picture of Lizz or Elizabeth in her mind now A lovely, attractive, clever girl that had not found her place or career in life before she disappeared.

'Oh, Nessa, with all this coming and going, I almost forget the reason I am here. Where are you, my dear friend?' She wept softly for a while.

Then she remembered the box of odds and ends that Agnes had given her and decided she should at least look at them before returning them.

She emptied out the box on the sofa beside her and started by dividing the items into postcards, letters, various pieces of paper and put the trinkets to one side.

The post cards were unusual in that they were mainly of famous sculptures held in different museums and art galleries around Europe. On each postcard there was only a line from poems that she recognised, no signature and no greeting. Strange, she mused. Elizabeth must have known the sender and they must have meant something to her if she had kept them in this memory box. None of them had been sent by post, there was no stamp on them. On the back of each was a simple line of poetry or a loving message, on three were written the years, 1993, 1994 and 1995. She jottted down the quotations and message on a page of her notebook and then considered the year that Elizabeth went missing, August 1995.

The letters had postmarks on them, she could not make out the dates, but she guessed they were local. The two letters only contained a single sheet of paper in each. They both looked like the ending of a letter. Maybe she had discarded the other pages, for some reason. They both contained the same sort of sentiment: 'You are mine forever and ever' and 'We

159

are meant for each other', 'a wonderful future ahead for us darling', there was no signature.

Did she have a romantic relationship with someone from the age of sixteen? That was likely now, she thought, after her conversation with Maria.

She looked at the other objects. The pieces of paper were also interesting. Small scraps really, with just one or two words on most, and one with a long sentence: 'forsaking all others I will be faithful onto thee'. What did they mean, or were they just the jottings of a lovesick teenager, Elizabeth herself or her beau?

They were all written in capital letters. The first scrap she looked at read: BEACH 4, another LAKE 6, KS 10, FH 6. They were all the same, a word and a number. She guessed these were places and times for meetings. There was also a bit of cheap jewellery, a ring with a glass stone a heavy silver charm bracelet, which Claire knew was valuable, and a pair of pearl earrings.

Enough for one night, she thought. Niall is coming and I can show him these and see what he thinks. She returned all the mementos to the box and yawned.

It was midnight and she fell into bed so weary and bone tired. She hoped sleep would come easily and it did.

Chapter 25

It was nearly ten o'clock when Claire awoke. She lay trying to remember the date and day it was. Her life was becoming strange and disoriented. She wondered when Niall would arrive and if there were any new developments.

Later she drove to the village and rang Niall. He would be at the cottage mid-afternoon and Inspector Savage would possibly be with him. Could she provide a bit of food for them, he wondered?

Claire smiled to herself. Did men always associate women with food? She decided to say hello to Joe and then go to the big town, Glencarr. There was no wine left either and she thought she would make a nice curry and get some beer too.

Joe enquired whether there was any news? He was looking a bit drawn these days and Claire wondered how healthy the man was. Mary was not there today so Claire left and drove to town.

By one o'clock she had her shopping done and decided to have a coffee and sandwich before starting back. She sat in a little café, looking out on the main street.

She was startled when she got a wave from someone she had just met. It was Mick! She smiled and waved back. He was just crossing the street and then entered a large hardware store that stocked animal feed.

She started to think about the life he and his sister led. It must be lonely, with just the two of them up there. You could hardly call poor Paddy good company, unfortunately. He needed care as would a young child.

She sighed and finished her coffee. As she walked back to the car park, she decided on another treat for Paddy. She knew that she would have to return home very soon. She found what she was looking for in a cost-price store and knew that Paddy would be delighted.

At four o'clock she had her curry ready and rice ready to cook. The fire was lit, and she sat down, still tired from her previous energetic day. She had the memory box ready to show Niall and wondered what he would make of her newly found information.

She was not sure if the next lesson with Paddy would be up the mountain or here. Andy would let her know. She put the items she had bought in town into the carryall just in case she forgot about them. Then she discovered some copybooks that she thought she had left for Paddy. But they were old ones, and she realised that she had taken them by mistake. Never mind, I can return them whenever.

There was a knock on the door at four-thirty and Niall and Aidan were on the doorstep. They looked rather bleary-eyed to Claire.

They made short work of the curry later and the beer too. They had been working long hours they told her. She refrained from asking for news. By now she knew that if there was any, it would have been announced immediately.

She felt downcast again until she remembered that she also had been busy, gathering information.

They sat at the table and she produced the box that Agnes had given her. She kept up a running commentary on her conversation with Agnes and then her meeting with Maria.

The two men listened and absorbed the new information. They were especially interested in Maria's version of events and her description of Elizabeth.

'It sounds like our Elizabeth was a woman of the world. It could be that she was not abducted at all, you know. I'd say she felt stifled in a small place like this, wouldn't you Niall?' Aidan turned over the postcards and read each line of poetry carefully.

'I could see that too. Her parents were also over-protective, I think. Couldn't wait to get away I'd say.'

'Yes Niall, but at the same time, she only had one more month to wait before spreading her wings. September would have seen a lot of that class drifting off to university and jobs. Most would be leaving Knocknabó, wouldn't they?'

'Yeah, you are right Claire. If she had lived that long there, she would surely have waited to leave in a proper manner and not have wanted to upset her parents, however fussy they were.

'That leaves the abduction theory, and if that's the case, I'd say the girl is dead.'

Claire's heart sank. Did he not realise how awful that sounded to herself and Niall; was he insensitive or did he just forget?

As though hearing her thoughts, Aidan apologised and hoped he had not diminished any hope they had. A case going back twenty-two years was a different matter, he thought.

At six o'clock Andy arrived without Paddy. It had gone late he explained, and they had had a hard day, cutting and loading up turf. Claire brought him in and introduced him to Aidan. He accepted a cup of tea and sat at the table with the men.

Talk turned again to Elizabeth and Niall asked Andy what he could remember of his cousin, if at all.

'Not that much I'm afraid. I was only about six and Paddy would have been about eight, I suppose. The only recollection I have, is of her red hair and the way Paddy used to love playing with it. We played games, hide and seek and if it was wet, we used to play in the barn sometimes. I was not up there that much. I still remember Mick shouting at us to 'get the hell out of that hay!' He laughed when he recalled it.

'Where were you on the night that Nessa collected the key to the cottage here?'

The question came like a bolt out of the blue and Andy was startled into confusion.

'Where was I? I was here in the village. I met Nessa earlier and she had missed the turn off to the cottage. It was a hellish night, rain pelting down. I was soaked after the walk home.'

'You gave her directions, didn't you?'

'Yes, I told her to drive a couple of miles further and she would be able to pick up the track.'

'But you were passing the first turn off yourself a couple of minutes later, why not get her to turn around and go back?' Aidan Savage gave the man his uncanny sideways look.

Andy got a bit flustered. 'I didn't think of that. Anyway, the road is narrow enough and if there was another car coming while she was doing a U turn, it could have caused an accident, couldn't it?'

'So, when you passed that original turn off, could you see her through the trees, her headlights, I mean?'

'No, I wasn't exactly gazing around me, the rain was blinding, and I had my head down.' He stared, puzzled at the detective.

'Are you seriously saying that I might have had something to do with the girl's disappearance?'

Claire broke in, 'of course not Andy. That was not the intention, was it, Aidan?' She glared at Savage.

'No, indeed not, but in every case, the exact whereabout of anybody near the crime scene would be of great interest.'

Niall grinned at him. 'Your dad already told us the time you arrived wet and bedraggled.'

Andy mockingly wiped his forehead. 'Do you realise how guilty you can make a person feel by firing questions at them like that? One more round and I'd be confessing to anything and everything.'

They all laughed a bit but then it petered out awkwardly.

'Do you believe that whoever took Nessa is from around here?' Andy looked in disbelief from one man to the other.

Aidan shook his head. 'I wish we could say for definite, the problem is, there is little to go on. That's why we are looking at all the missing cases in the area around this county.'

'Well, your honour, if I have your permission, I must return to the farm. My aunt is returning tomorrow, and I will leave in the morning to pick her up. We are expecting the vet first thing to dose a few of the sick ewes.' Andy pushed back his chair and got to his feet.

Aidan laughed and got up to shake his hand. 'Sorry if you felt you were being interrogated, Andy. It was lovely meeting you and I hope you won't hold my questioning habit against me.'

'Not at all, I'll be on the lookout for you from now on though!'

Andy said goodnight to them all and Claire went to the door with him.

166

'I'll go up tomorrow if you like, I have something special for Paddy.'

'That's fine Claire. I should be back with Margie early afternoon, hopefully, if there are no delays at the hospital. I need to help dad for a couple of hours. Claire walked down the path with him. 'Don't be upset by that inquisition, I'm sure he did not mean to upset you. It's just his way.'

'Once a policeman, always a policeman,' Andy quipped. He got into the old farm jeep and drove away.

She returned to a quiet kitchen. The men were drinking more beer and looking through the box again and Niall was flicking through Paddy's books.

'I had better return that box to Agnes tomorrow, are you finished with it, boys?

Niall nodded. Aidan lifted his head. 'You can also do something else for us, seeing as you are good at gathering information, Claire. Will you ask Agnes about her memories of the night that Elizabeth did not return home? There may be nothing further, but hope springs eternal, you know.

Aidan, having decided to stay over, Claire made up the bed in the loft that once was Nessa's. She then left the men together and went off to bed. She felt exhausted. She never heard them going to bed as she was out like a light.

167

Chapter 26

The men had already left when Claire rose. By the looks of it, they did not have breakfast either. She thought they could have waited until she got up and told them her plans for the day. She had a shower and felt better. As she dried her hair, she suddenly had a longing for home and see her mother and father. I'll go tomorrow, she decided. It was time, she was not going anywhere in this situation and she needed her life to get back to some sort of normality.

She had a leisurely breakfast and looked through Elizabeth's box one last time. The silver bracelet was really pretty, the sort of thing you might get for a birthday present.

She met Agnes as the woman returned from her routine trip to the church. Claire got out of the car where she had been waiting and walked up the path with the box.

Nora was with her today and invited her in for a cup of coffee. They sat in the front room and Agnes took the box from Claire.

'Thank you for sharing that, Agnes. I was admiring that charm bracelet she had. Did she get it for a birthday present?'

Agnes opened the box and took out the bracelet.

'No, I don't think so. I don't know where she got it. We didn't give it to her anyway, must have been one of the girls. She only ever wore a cross and chain her dad gave her.'

Coming into the room with the tray of coffee, Nora craned her neck to see the bracelet and Agnes held it up to her.

She put down the tray on the coffee table and took the bracelet up, 'Holy God! That is pure silver and quite a weight. It must have been expensive, very expensive. I doubt that the girls could have afforded anything so grand.'

She asked if Nessa's brother had any news? Claire shook her head and said she was feeling like it was a bad dream.

'I need to go home to my parents and family; I need their support and a return to normality. I feel helpless here and I cannot contribute much to poor Niall. I don't know how he is coping or the rest of the family either.'

Both women murmured their agreement. It was not looking good. They both had spoken of this at length by themselves and did not believe that Nessa was anywhere near here. Her car was the clue, they thought. Somebody hijacked her and took her too, but the car must have been the thing they wanted.

'Before I go, Agnes and Nora, would you mind very much if you just went over that last night when Elizabeth did not return. Can you just go over the entire evening with me from the time Elizabeth left the house?'

Agnes looked a bit puzzled for a moment. 'I've gone over it so often in my head, it's like recalling a dream at this stage.'

'Just give it another try Aggie,' urged Nora.

'There was nothing much out of the ordinary. I felt at the time, that she was really…', she stopped and searched for the word that would describe her last time with her precious daughter, 'content, that's what she was, totally content, I thought. I knew that she must have decided on the career she planned and was relieved.'

'Did she tell you what it was that she decided to do with her life?'

'No, it was always going to be something to do with children, I think. For a couple of months before, there was a restlessness about her and a strange tension in the house. I thought it was nerves about the exams, but sure, she loved school and was top of the class, why would she be nervous about them? When the results did come out, she had got fantastic points and could have done anything she wanted. No, there was a change in her that last week and all I can say is, she was a contented girl, and all that old tension was gone, even her father noticed it. It was as if she had made up her mind about something, I'm sure now that it was what she was planning to do with her life.'

Nora nodded. 'Sure, it's a difficult time for students, deciding what they're going to do. It was more difficult back twenty years ago. She would have had to move away to go to university anyway or teacher training college. Who knows what she would have chosen?'

Claire finished her coffee and went to get up. 'Was there anyone here that night Agnes, while she was at the school hall with the other girls?'

Agnes thought for a moment. 'The only person to call, after her uncle Joe left, was Margie. She wanted a couple of days away with Paddy and wondered if Elizabeth could come, as Paddy adored her. It might be a long time before they had her to themselves if she went to college and left the village. Paddy was always easier to manage if Elizabeth was there.'

Nora passed the woman a tissue to catch the tears that were never far away, filling up Agnes' eyes.

'I remember the night so well too. My Maria came in and she was totally shattered. They had been so busy that Thursday and the whole crowd of them had hair appointments booked from early the next morning, and they were getting their nails done too. I think that added to the excitement. It was going to be another long day and night. Maria had a shower and went straight to bed. For her to be in bed before eleven was something, I can tell you!'

'How long would it have taken her to walk from the school hall?'

'Only ten to twelve minutes for Maria, and ten more for Elizabeth, I reckon.'

'Did Margie stay waiting for her to come home, Agnes? Claire had sat down again.

'No, she had to get back to Paddy. She must have left around ten-thirty. I thought she might meet her on the way, but she didn't, it seems.' Agnes wiped her eyes again.

'What about Joe? Was he there when Margie was there?'

'Ah no, he was just checking with Andrew about the coming fishing weekend they were planning, and which of course, never happened after all.'

Claire stood up again. 'I have taken up so much of your time, ladies. I thank you for all your kindness to me and apologise for reviving painful memories. I know that the detective wants every little scrap of information and is somehow connecting Nessa to your daughter and the other missing women.'

They all embraced and hoped that good news would come soon. They hoped that Claire would settle back in her job and hoped to see her again in happier times.

Claire traveled back to Kilshee digesting the conversation she had with the two women. She stopped at the village store and saw Mary serving. Joe must be out on deliveries, she guessed.

'I must get a few chocolate bars for Paddy, I'm going up after lunch, before it gets too dark. I just hate November Mary, it's dreary, isn't it?'

'It surely is that. Andy went off early enough to get Margie. I hope to God, she is not coming back too soon. She had a stent put in and seemingly the consultant is happy with her. She had a blockage in one artery, that was why she was so exhausted all the time. Andy was worried about her.'

'Lucky woman, that they got it in time, Mary. Those operations are wonderful I believe.'

'Oh yes, it'll be back to business now. That woman has always had amazing energy, she'd be equal to any man for hard work.'

'She is lucky to have Andy as well as Mick. It's a big farm Mary. Will Andy be content to settle here do you think? He seems to have loved New Zealand.'

Mary nodded. 'He doesn't say much, our Andy. I have a suspicion that Margie had something to do with Andy coming back. I wouldn't be surprised if she asked him to.'

'Why not ask him then? Mick surely is a partner by now too?'

'It's easy to see that you are not from a farming background Claire. These things are not discussed openly; questions about land and who has rights cause great suspicion. I want to know nothing even though I grew up there; I'm still feeling upset about my brother Hugh.'

'What does Joe think of it all?'

'He doesn't know about Hugh, so he just thinks she and her brother have sorted it out. That's why he

173

does not understand why our Andy is bothered to work there with no entitlement.'

Claire left then to go and have lunch before setting off for the farm. She would never understand this great hunger that Irish people had for land. She stopped to ring Niall before leaving the village. They were in Killarney and hoped to be back that evening. She was told not to worry about food. Well, that would be nice, she thought. If they eat before getting here, there is plenty of food in the fridge that I can have.

Chapter 27

Claire sat and enjoyed her sandwiches and tea. Asking questions was hungry work she found. Afterwards she went upstairs and packed her bag and tidied up the room. She would do the rest of the cleaning and tidying tomorrow and wash the bed linen and towels and generally leave the cottage as she found it.

At two o'clock, there was a knock on the door. Coming downstairs she thought it must be Niall and was surprised to find Paddy and Mick on the doorstep.

Mick quickly explained that he had an appointment that afternoon and did not want to leave Paddy alone. Andy would be travelling home by now, he hoped but there could be traffic delays.

It was no problem for Claire, and she welcomed Paddy in and told Mick that she would drive him back later, if that was alright.

'There won't be any need I'm sure Claire, I expect Andy will call for him. I let him know that Paddy would be here.'

Paddy made himself at home and opened his plastic file and emptied it on the kitchen table.

'Ce'h, lukahmawok, Pa'h mmbsee.'

Claire took the proffered copy book up and admired his pictures. 'You certainly have been very busy Paddy.'

'I have something new for you today. I think you will like what I bought.'

She took out the poster paints and brushes and a big painting pad that she had got at the cost price store.

Laying newspapers on the table she began the task of introducing Paddy to mixing colours and applying them on paper.

The lad was fascinated and very eager to try it. She taught him how to make other colours with the primary colours she had bought.

'Now Paddy try mixing the blue and yellow and see what you get.'

It was a concentrated lesson. Paddy learned quickly and was totally absorbed in the mixing of paint and achieving the different colours.

The flew time by and she made tea and produced the chocolate bars. Paddy hardly noticed them he was so absorbed.

She lit the fire as he worked and silently watched the man. She treated him like a child she knew, but he was a man and strong at that. He had his uncle's physique; both were tall and muscular, the right physique for farmers, she thought.

What would happen to him in later years, she wondered? She knew that he would be unable to care for himself and would always need supervision. She guessed that Margie was in her late fifties, Mick looked younger than his sister. Thankfully, she had her stent put in now, she knew from experience that it was a successful procedure and could be repeated if necessary.

She went behind the man and looked over his shoulder. He was drawing again, with the paint brush. He had a recognisable cottage there and that dark shadow must be a mountain she guessed. There was blue in the sky too she saw and blue underneath the mountain, if it was that.

'That's wonderful Paddy, is that your house and the mountain behind?'

Paddy nodded and kept painting in the shapes he had made.

She leaned forward and pointed to the blue under the mountain. 'Is that the lake up behind where you live, Paddy?'

'Ess, Ce'h,' and there followed a long "Paddy sentence", that she could not understand.

He was putting a lot of effort into the darkness under the lake. She thought she saw a tractor emerging.

'Oh, that's Mick on the tractor, right?'

Paddy laughed loudly. 'Da Pa'h, Ce'h.'

'You Paddy? I didn't know you could drive a tractor.'

Paddy turned to look at her. 'Evundrva tako, Ce'h.' He said this so seriously that Claire believed him.

'Yes, of course, on a farm, everyone drives a tractor. Does your Mum drive it too?'

Paddy nodded.

Still, she was surprised. She had thought that his mother would not allow it, being so protective of him and seeing as how her husband had died as a result of a tractor accident.

Then his attention turned something else. He was pouring out the red paint into one of the little containers provided with the kit. He proceeded to draw that same little car that he always drew. He had it up between the tractor and the lake. It was totally in the wrong place, but there was no way that Claire would correct him. This was his drawing and painting, and it would not do for her to try and influence him.

Again, she offered him a chocolate bar.

'Have a rest now, Paddy, you have worked so hard this afternoon and you need a break.'

He stopped and opened the chocolate bar and ate it, all the while looking at his painting. He was obviously smitten.

'I'd say that the painting is finished now, Paddy. Will we leave it dry? It takes a while to dry it but otherwise you will smudge it and make it messy if you try and move it while it is still wet.'

He nodded and smiled at her.

'Ess Ce'h, Pa'h wa'h teepeeze.'

She smiled and put on the kettle. Now he took his copy book and started with the colouring pencils. She would wait a while until the painting was dry and she could give it to him to bring home.

He was working again. Head down, stopping only to take a slurp of tea and a bite of the bar. He certainly has concentration she thought.

She told Paddy that she would bring the wet painting up tomorrow or he could collect it if he was coming here. Then she remembered her plan to leave tomorrow. She felt reluctant to try and explain that she was leaving. Better to leave that to Andy, she thought. She would drop it up before she left for good, she decided.

'Time to go home, I think, Paddy'.

He was still hunched over the table colouring with his pencils. As he lifted his head to look at her there was a knock on the door. She opened it, expecting Andy but was surprised to see Niall and his friend Aidan standing there.

They came into the warm and welcoming heat of the kitchen. Paddy looked alarmed when he saw the stranger with Niall whom he had met.

Aidan came forward and offered his hand and Paddy shyly took it. The traffic was heavy, and the men had made an earlier start than first intended.

'Well boys, I have not made any dinner, so are you starving, or can you wait? Andy will be here shortly to collect Paddy. There is a good Indian takeaway in Knocknabó, what about getting a nice hot curry?

'Tell you what Claire, we'll go and collect a curry for the three of us. Is that alright?'

They sat down in front of the fire and talked about curries and what the three of them liked.

Paddy went back to his drawing and paid no attention to the others. He was totally absorbed.

It was thirty minutes later when Andy called at the door. He greeted the other two men and told Claire that he wanted to get Margie back to the house as quickly as possible, as stormy weather was expected. He apologised for the delay. The consultant had been late coming to see Margie before she could be discharged and then they had got stuck in traffic.

Again, as they went to leave the cottage, Paddy paused by the print on the wall and uttered his strange mixed-up language. He pointed to it and back to his painting on the table.

Claire nodded understandingly and opened the door and tried to usher him out. He stayed and kept up his chat. He became impatient at her inability to understand him and she remembered the tantrum he had thrown before with Andy.

'It's alright Paddy, I know what you're saying.'

The man shook his head vehemently and repeated the litany and added "Ce'h, Ce'h". He seemed to forget that he had an audience with the two men behind them. He pointed to the picture and pulled it off the wall and thrust it under Claire's nose.

For the first time, Claire felt fear. He had a look in his eyes that was unlike his usual soft and docile look. It suddenly dawned on her that he could be violent, and she was startled.

Niall came forward to look at the print now. Paddy took a step backwards and thrust it at him. He appeared to become his usual gentle self. He walked out the door and got into Margie's car without another word.

Niall raised his eyebrows at Claire, and she shrugged her shoulders and followed Andy out.

Claire leaned in to ask Margie how she was feeling and got a warm smile in reply. 'Never better, Claire. Thank you for all your minding of Paddy.'

Andy said he would be in touch tomorrow and waved goodbye.

Claire returned to the cottage and found the men around the table drinking coffee and looking at Paddy's drawings.

Chapter 28

When the two men had left to go to Knocknabó, Claire stacked more turf on the fire and cleared the table of the paint and drawings that Paddy had done. She forgot the episode of the print as she worked swiftly. Here was her day almost gone and she had not managed to leave to go home. Well, tomorrow she would definitely leave. She would go and say her goodbyes to Joe and Mary and explain to Andy. He could explain to Paddy. At the same time, she felt reluctant to go now and wondered if she would be encouraged by the men.

They all enjoyed their curries and Niall had brought more beer to have with them. The rain was pounding against the windows as they sat and ate. It was a cosy setting in the little cottage.

Afterwards they sat in front of the fire drinking the beer. Niall sat on the sofa beside Claire and the detective sat in the old, battered armchair.

'Did you not think it strange when Paddy got upset, Claire?' Aidan asked quietly when there was a pause in the conversation.

'Well, for a moment. He nearly had a tantrum before about it. I think it is just frustration at not being understood. Poor lad.'

Niall looked at her. 'Claire, we were worried about that outburst. What do you know about the lad, really?'

She looked at them in surprise. After considering the question for a few moments, she mused out loud, 'Well, I suppose I know nothing about him really, except that he is usually very gentle and childlike. Tonight's outburst did knock me for six. It is not like his usual behaviour, believe me.

Niall coughed and took a drink of beer. 'Claire, Aidan and I have been discussing things, and we both think you should leave here as soon as possible and return home to your folk.'

Claire looked at them in surprise. 'You do? Why now, at this time, may I ask?' She was not going to tell them that she had already decided to leave the next day.

'There are some results coming in and we don't think it safe for you to be here,' Aidan stated.

'Well, you must know something new then, won't you at least let me in on it?'

Niall again gave that little nervous cough. 'Claire, it's better that you know nothing. Everything is supposition, at the moment, nothing more. We would feel more relaxed if we knew that you were out of danger.'

'Sorry lads, that won't wash. I don't feel in any danger, especially not from poor Paddy. I have been busy too, asking questions.'

Aidan and Niall looked at each other and both sighed. 'Let's hear what you have learned from your activities Claire.'

They ended up that night, sitting at the kitchen table and Claire recounted all her meetings with Agnes, Nora and Maria. She told them of Agnes's last evening with her daughter and of her feeling that Elizabeth was totally content and at ease with herself.

The men made notes and they all took part in theorising about what was going on that evening. When Claire told them that the last visitor with Agnes was Margie, they were startled.

'If she left at the time Agnes says, she should have seen Elizabeth on the road, walking home, unless she met someone else before that and accepted a lift.

They sat in silence. At last Claire asked the men why they thought she might be in danger here?

Aidan closed his notebook and looked directly at Claire, not his sideways look.

'Claire, certain things have surfaced that we have not confided in you for obvious reasons. That missed call on Nessa's phone was traced to this locality, well, within ten or fifteen miles or so, the nearest transmitter is beyond this village, the other interesting thing is, your number and Nessa's were in touch some nights after Nessa's missed call to you. How do you explain that? Is there something you are not telling us?'

Claire looked at them in amazement. 'You think I was in touch with Nessa and didn't tell you?'

Niall spread his hands, 'the two numbers came up together and we can't explain it Claire.'

'Well, I can't either. Sorry, but I was not in touch with Nessa. I would be over the moon if I had been and would have told you straight away Niall. What on earth are you thinking?'

Niall nodded his head and looked miserable. 'I know, Claire. I believe you would.'

'Wait! Have you got the date these two calls came through on?'

Aidan opened his notebook again and told her. Claire thought for a few moments. 'There was one night when I was not in possession of my phone, no, that's wrong, two nights. After the missed call, I gave Joe and Mary my phone in case Nessa phoned again and the second night was when Paddy took my phone from the car and brought it home with him, innocently enough, as I told Andy he could play with it.'

'That explains it then. It seems that your mobile and Nessa's were at the same location that night.'

Claire could hardly believe her ears. 'How can you be sure of that?'

Niall told her that it had taken some time to trace the first call but when the two were used almost simultaneously, the cell tower picked up.

'What does that mean and how could that happen?'

'Perhaps by someone 'playing' with them Claire?'

Chapter 29

The night continued for the three people in the cottage. The beer being finished, coffee was brewed at regular intervals until almost three o'clock in the morning.

As Claire later stumbled to bed, her head in a whirl from all the intense questions and wild suppositions, she knew that although exhausted, she would never sleep. The men insisted that they needed sleep and would continue the conversation the next day.

Claire lay in the dark room, listening to the wind and rain hammer the windows downstairs, trying to make sense of the various findings of the men.

At one stage, all Paddy's copybooks were pulled out of his file and examined as was his painting.

'It's a very simple painting, isn't it? I mean, a child would paint a house like that, not a bit sophisticated or adult, is it? Niall turned the painting every which way.

Aidan then took the painting. Then he went and took the print off the wall that had started Paddy's agitation.

'I think that Paddy was drawing this view; the mountain, bogland and a lake then the house further down, though how the car comes into it I don't know. And the tractor; obviously there is one up on the farm?' He turned to Claire as he asked this.

'Yes of course, I've seen the uncle driving it, but Paddy informed me recently that he is the one driving the tractor, whether or not he does drive it I can't tell. We could ask Andy I suppose. But why is the red car above it, it's completely out of place, isn't it?

Niall made a strange discovery but also a sinister one; the little red car that Paddy was always drawing was scrutinised further, with the help of a magnifying glass. The number plate seemed to be a replica of Nessa's car, even though the numbers were a bit difficult to see, and some were backwards, it was an English registered number as Nessa had registered it when she bought it from her brother. The earlier copy books were also checked; at first it was only the red car was drawn, and then in later copybooks, the numbers appeared.

That discovery really stumped the three and a long silence ensued. How did Paddy have access to that knowledge? What did it mean? Had he seen it before, maybe in July when she was in the cottage for a month? They thought that it was the most probable answer, Nessa had been there and often left the car when she went off sketching. Most people in Kilshee would have been familiar with her car.

Then Niall mentioned how red-haired people seemed to dominate Paddy's drawing. Claire smiled and said yes and said that no doubt it was her, though it could have been Andy too.

'No, it's definitely a female head.'

Claire laughed, 'yes and he always says I'm pretty.'

Then the smile died on her face. 'Oh, my goodness! I assumed it was 'pretty' he was saying. He was always insistent, 'Bitty', he always said, and Andy interpreted it as pretty, but supposing it was 'Betty?'

'But who is Betty when she is at home?' Aidan looked intently at Claire.

'Elizabeth was called a number of variations of that name, Liz, Lizzie, Betty.'

'The girl who has been missing for twenty-two years?' Niall asked incredulously, 'but, that's so long ago and Paddy was only, what age?'

'About eight years old,' Claire said quietly. 'Paddy was very fond of her and she looked after him quite a bit. Andy said that Paddy loved playing with her hair.'

'Right, that settles it. Tomorrow we must get Andy in and talk to him.'

Claire lay awake wondering what would happen next. There must be an innocent explanation for all these things. Paddy was a child in a man's body, although an obviously strong individual. What would poor Andy think about all this. She desperately wanted to shield Paddy from any stress and questioning. His mother knew that he could not cope with stress as did Claire.

The whole scenario was like something out of a horror movie and she just wished there were a way of rolling back time and that Nessa and herself were arranging a different holiday in a different place, far away from this village and the people she had come to feel at home with and love.

Eventually she slept fitfully, and her dreams were filled with figures in masks, most of them monsters, moving nearer and nearer to her, until she awoke wet with sweat and panting.

She lay still and tried to become calm. It was only a dream and she relaxed a bit until she remembered the findings of the previous night. She sat up in bed and listened. There were sounds coming from downstairs. Then she realised the men must be up already and threw on her dressing gown and went downstairs.

They were finishing their breakfast and Claire was shocked to hear the time. I must have slept after all, she thought.

'Why did you not call me, it's almost eleven.'

'Why would we do that? It was a very late night, and you were exhausted.'

Claire sat down and Niall poured her a cup of tea. She declined a cooked breakfast but took a piece of toast offered.

As she was eating it, a knock came to the door. She looked up in surprise. Niall smiled at her and said, we have our visitor. I went into the village earlier and asked him to come and see us asap.'

Aidan answered the door and led Andy into the kitchen. The man looked bewildered and smiled when he saw a disheveled Claire, just obviously out of bed.

'Well lads, I came just as soon as I could and I made the excuses to my employer, as requested. How can I help you?'

Claire excused herself. She would not be able to think straight until she had a shower. When she re-emerged the two men were explaining to Andy the significance of Paddy's artwork and copybooks.

She went upstairs and dressed, and then dried her hair. That felt much better, she thought. Now to go and help out poor Andy, who must be puzzled about what was being spoken about.

She descended the stairs and heard Andy remonstrate strongly; 'Paddy is an innocent and is not capable of violence, surely you can see that?'

The men brought his attention to the fuss he made over the print on the wall by the hall door. Then they showed him the car with the number plates, unnoticed before this.

Andy was stumped. 'I have no idea how he would know the number plates of Nessa's car. It is only recently that I became aware that he knew numbers. Maybe he saw the car when she was here last?'

'How often does he come to the village here, Andy?'

'Well, it's not often at all. But maybe he has what you call it, a photographic memory?'

'Alright, perhaps, now look at the print and then his painting which he did yesterday, what can you tell us Andy?' Aidan pushed both items in front of Andy.

Andy looked at both. 'Yes, I can see a similarity for sure. That is the area beyond the house and there is a lake there, like in the painting and print. Maybe he was painting the print by memory. He was quite excited when he saw it first, wasn't he Claire?'

'He certainly was, and not *just* excited, I think. We were inclined to dismiss it and paid no attention to him and then he had a bit of a tantrum, didn't he, Andy?'

The men continued to question Andy about any violent tendencies that Paddy might have; had he ever witnessed any violence from him up to this time?

'Only the usual frustrations that would drive anyone mad. It's twice as frustrating for him as he cannot communicate his feelings. The idea that you would think he could harbour violent feelings towards a virtual stranger, like Nessa, is totally over the top.'

Claire made a pot of coffee and they sat in silence considering what came next.

It was finally agreed that nothing should be said to anyone at the farm about Paddy, and his drawings that had caused all these suspicions; more digging was needed.

Claire remembered last night's theory that 'Bitty' meant Betty. She asked Andy what he had called his cousin.

He raised his eyebrows at that change of direction. 'Lordy, you're only going back more than twenty years, lads. I was only six when she went off. I called her 'Izzy' as far as I can remember.'

When Claire suggested that 'Bitty' might have meant Betty, Andy was sceptical. He doubted that Paddy meant Betty, after all, it was so long ago, wasn't it?

Detective Savage asked what sort of child Paddy was, was he tall for his age, what about his strength?

Andy's eyes widened in disbelief. 'You are now suspecting the lad of her disappearance? This is really scraping the barrel, isn't it? Yes, he was tall for his age and he was bigger and stronger than me and he still is, but that means nothing. His mental age is about eight or nine, isn't it, Claire?'

Claire nodded. She was ashamed of the questions that were being shot at Andy and wanted to protect him.

'Has he ever overcome you, Andy?' Niall asked this softly.

Andy paused and the silence grew. 'Well, there was one time when he grew frustrated at not being allowed on the tractor, he must have been about fourteen at the time, and he picked me up and threw me up on top of a hayrick.' He smiled ruefully as he recounted this.

Claire laughed out loud. 'I'd love to have seen *that'* she chuckled.

The two men did not laugh however, and that awkward silence again descended.

That reminded Claire about Paddy assertion that he had been the one driving the tractor in the painting.

'Does Paddy drive the tractor Andy?'

Andy spread his hands and explained that he had once taught the lad to drive as he was desperate to learn. 'I never told Margie, so please don't go telling her now. It was only a couple of times. He would never ask to drive it if Mick were about.'

They all absorbed this other bit of news silently.

'If that's all, lads, I really must go now, it's a busy time with cutting turf, mending fences and checking pregnant ewes.'

'Before you go Andy, and again thank you for coming here and submitting to this interrogation, there is just one other thing: what sort of people are his parents?'

'His father died in a tractor accident when he was only a baby, Mick is his uncle and Margie's brother, they are a bit, what you'd call odd; they don't communicate as much as you'd expect. I'm not sure exactly about their personalities. I get on with both.

They don't live in the same house of course so I usually get my orders from Margie.'

Claire felt she should ask a question now, that she always wanted to ask and had not get the opportunity.

'Andy, did Margie have anything to do with you coming back here?'

Andy sat back down and looked down at his hands. 'It's a bit complicated Claire. She is worried about Paddy being able to manage on his own, understandable enough, I suppose. She asked if I could come back and work for her and help with Paddy. He will eventually inherit the farm of course, and there is no way he could run it.'

'What about her brother Mick? He has spent many years up there working, hasn't he, nothing about his being made her partner? That to me would make the most sense, don't you think?' Aidan turned to Niall with this question.

Niall laughed and spread his hands out. 'Land again! There is neither sense nor reason when it comes to land being left in a will.'

Andy left shortly after this and the men left to go to the nearest station and check any further news available.

Chapter 30

Claire realised her plan to return home had again been postponed. She felt that she should be helping to dig around a bit, even if it were only to deflect their awful suspicions about Paddy. He did not deserve this, and she knew that if Niall and Aidan knew him like she did, they would not entertain such thoughts. She was afraid that the men might want to question Paddy and thought that it would be detrimental to him.

She knew what she had to do right now. The simplest remedy for her: the sea. After the ten-minute drive, she was striding along the seashore, hair blowing every which way, the salty air filling her lungs.

The beach was deserted on this chilly morning. Clouds scudded across the sky and seagulls wheeled above, dipping down occasionally to find something to eat. She was warm by the time she reached the end of the beach and sat for some minutes on the flat stone she had sat on before, when she had found Mary crying. It seemed like months had elapsed and it was only days. How was it that time seemed to be able to bend and last forever, and at other times, it flew like the wind and could not be held back. She looked back to the day she had arrived here, it now seemed like years ago, or did she mean moments? It seemed all the same to her suddenly. Where are you, Nessa? Will you please lead us to you, please? Life won't be able to move until you do. We will all be stuck in this warp, unable to think or move ahead. How can we get back to normal? Nessa if you can hear my thoughts, do something.

She got up and started her return walk, the wind behind her now and gently pushing her back. She reached her car and turned on the heat. Her extremities were freezing and her face. She sat and let her thoughts settle. Then her eyes fell on to Paddy's file on the passenger seat. She meant to return them today. She again took out the earlier copybooks and scrutinised them. The answer lies with Paddy, she suddenly thought. What does the child/man know? He was so agitated about the print on the wall. Why? What did it signify to him and how could she find out?

After lunch there was still no sign of Niall and she drove to the village for some provisions. The shop was busy now and both Joe and Mary and Lisa were serving. She picked up what she needed and would have left except that Mary beckoned her over to the coffee corner. She was relieved, she had hoped for a quiet word with Mary.

Mary told her that Andy was worried about the police questioning, and frightened that they would terrify Paddy. Claire nodded and told the woman that if she had anything to do with it, that would not happen. She explained that some of the man's drawings were strange. Then she took out the print to show Mary. This was why she had come after all.

'Mary, does this print mean anything to you? It seems to upset Paddy, each time he sees it, he gets over-excited.'

Mary studied the print. 'Why that's the mountain beyond the farmhouse, where I grew up. It's lovely, mainly bogland of course, but there is a lake there and the streams flow from the surrounding mountain down into it. It's beautiful in summer and we used to swim there when we were kids. Freezing, but we never minded that.' She smiled fondly at the recollection.

'Why would it agitate Paddy so much, Mary?'

'I have no idea, love, maybe it's just that he recognises it?'

'No, I think it is more than that Mary. Each time he comes to the cottage it happens and he did a painting of it yesterday.' She took the folded and now, dry painting from the file and showed it to Mary.

'Oh, he is quite good, isn't he? You can see that it is the same picture, except for the tractor and car.'

She bent to study the car and then looked up at Claire. 'Good God! Doesn't that look like your friend's car?'

Claire nodded and whispered to Mary, 'he even has the correct number plate on it.'

Mary stared open-mouthed at her. 'I didn't know he could understand numbers and letters, Claire.'

'This is why the two guards are perplexed and wonder what else poor Paddy knows. Mary, could you ask Andy to bring Paddy down this afternoon before night falls, if possible, and bring him here so I can have a quiet word with him alone. I don't want the two guards firing questions at him, I know that will scare him?'

Mary nodded her head. 'I will contact him after lunch and tell him to do that. You can fill him in on the details. I don't want to tell Andy on the phone, and I think it's better if Margie doesn't know. She might stop him coming.'

Claire felt relief. If there was something to convey to Niall, she would do it. To change the subject, she asked about Joe and how he was keeping?

Mary grimaced and said his blood pressure was still too high and he was due for a checkup in a couple of days again. He was to have a stress test, whatever that involved, she said. Claire could see that the woman was worried.

'If there is anything I can do, Mary, like drop you into the hospital or run errands, just say the word.'

'Andy will take a few days off if necessary, don't you worry. He has already spoken to Margie about it. How long is Niall going to stay here, do you think?'

'I don't really know; he doesn't say much. I know that there are different aspects of the case that they do not discuss with me and I understand that. I just want to help all I can and pass any bits and pieces of information to them that might prove fruitful.'

There was no further communication with the two men. Claire made a casserole and put it in the oven to slowcook at four o'clock. Then she took Paddy's file and drove to the village.

Mary brought her into the kitchen and made a cup of tea for both. At four twenty, Andy came through the inner door from the shop with Paddy in tow. The man was delighted and surprised to see Claire there. After Paddy had a cup of tea and the usual chocolate bar, Andy made to leave the kitchen. Claire stopped him and told him he should stay and help, if possible but let her to the talking. He nodded and sat over by the Aga, reading the paper.

Claire took out all the copybooks and painting and immediately Paddy grabbed the colouring pencils and took one of the books. Claire opened the painting again and spread it out on the table.

'This is really a wonderful painting, Paddy. Can you tell me a little bit about it? He paused in what he was doing and beamed at her.

'About this car, Paddy. Have you seen it about the village?'

Paddy shook his head and resumed his colouring.

Claire reached over from where she sat opposite and took his hand. 'Paddy, I think this is my friend's car. Did you know Nessa, who used to stay in the cottage?'

Paddy frowned and again shook his head and resumed his colouring.

Claire sighed. 'Paddy, Nessa was my friend and I loved her. She came here a few weeks ago and then she disappeared. Do you understand? My friend just vanished, and I am very sad for her. I miss her and I do not know where to find her.' Claire looked hopefully at the man.

'Paw Ce'h. Sa' and miz fwen.'

'Yes Paddy, and this car', she pointed again to the red car in the painting, 'this car, belongs to Nessa, so I want to find this car, do you understand?'

Paddy stopped his work and looked at the painting and the car and looked at Claire, he was frowning.

'Fwen cah?'

'Paddy do you know where this car is?'

'Ca'h aw gonnow. Monna.'

He shook his head and resumed his drawing. Now the same little car was appearing under his hand. His tongue sat on his lip as bent even closer and in the numbers of the car appeared again though minutely.

Andy approached the table and looked at the drawing. Very quietly he spoke to the man. 'You are brilliant at your numbers Paddy and your drawing, but can you tell us where the car went? Did you take it?'

Paddy laughed then and shook his head. 'Noh Pah, Dee. Monna.'

Claire looked at Andy in desperation. 'Is he saying what I think he is saying? Monster? A monster took Nessa's car?'

Andy looked sadly at Claire. 'If only we could get inside his mind. I think if he knew more, he would tell us. That seems to be the extent of his knowledge.'

Claire had an idea. 'What about if we went up to that place in the painting, the mountain and lake, and see if he can remember anything else, Andy.'

Andy thought about that. 'It might be worth trying, but I'd like to go when there is nobody about, he always clams up when his mother or Mick are about.'

They left it at that, and Andy agreed to find a way to bring Claire up with Paddy and himself.

When she reached the cottage, she was happy to see Niall's car. As she entered, the comforting smell of beef casserole met her, and Niall greeted her.

As they waited for the potatoes to cook, Niall gave her his news. The remains of a missing woman had been found in a shallow grave about twenty miles away. She had been reported missing a couple of weeks ago. Claire was shocked that she had not heard about it. Niall hastened to tell her that it was not Nessa.

'Do they think it may be connected to all the other cases?'

'We must not assume that they will all be connected Claire. People go missing every day of the week. The forensics are working on it now. It could have been a suicide, who knows? Aidan is up there now and will keep us posted.'

Claire digested this. She told him about her session with Paddy and explaining about Nessa and the car he was always drawing. Niall laughed dryly when he heard Paddy's explanation of what happened the red car.

'Monster? That's a good one, must be lots here.'

Claire agreed that Paddy's version was childish.

'If he knew something Niall, I think he would have said more, to explain, you know?'

Niall left the cottage at nine to go and phone Aidan and perhaps drive to Knocknabó to have a chat with the guards there. Something might turn up with this latest find. At some stage, the killer would make a mistake, if it were the same person responsible for all the missing women. They began to think they were invincible when nothing happened after some time had passed. He said a silent prayer as he drove that his sister might still be found safe, although his hopes were dwindling fast and Aidan had warned him that it was unrealistic to keep hoping, but how could he not?

Chapter 31

Claire was feeling so tired that she decided to call it a day and prepared to go to bed. Niall now had his own key, and she didn't have to worry about that.

As she ascended the stairs to the loft there was a sudden knocking on the door. She paused and wondered if he had forgotten his key and retraced her steps. As she was about the open the door, she remembered Aidan's warning.

'Who is it?' She suddenly felt fear and knew it could not be Niall.

The knocking continued and then she heard a tap on the window. Moving over to look her heart nearly stopped. A face was pressed against the glass. At first, she could not recognise it, then a big beaming smile showed it was Paddy.

'Oh Paddy!' She opened the door, and the man came into the kitchen. 'You frightened me Paddy, why are you here at this time, it's late and I was just going to bed.'

Paddy grabbed her hands and started his long rambling sentence which Claire could not understand.

He kept pointing to the print on the wall When she kept shaking her head and asking him to slow down, he stopped suddenly and said quite slowly, 'Ce'h's fwen, Ezzy, comet Pah, Ce'h.'

'Now Paddy? It's too late, maybe tomorrow?'

Again, that determined and obdurate tone and facial expression appeared. 'Now Ce'h, munbe now.'

As she continued to look doubtful, he stepped forward and scooped her up and threw her over his shoulder as if she were a bag of coal. He rushed out the door with her struggling and shouting.

'Let me down, Paddy, we'll talk, please.' She banged with her fists against his back to no avail.

She was bundled into the passenger seat of the old black farm jeep and immediately Paddy was in the front seat and the car took off with a suddenness that threw Claire against the dashboard.

Paddy drove silently and fast and Claire knew as she tried to straighten up in the seat that she could not open the door and throw herself out; it was locked, and all she could do, was to wait and see where they were going. Part of her was terrified but at the back of her mind, her brain was telling her that Paddy was not capable of violence.

Soon it became clear that they were heading towards the farm. She breathed slowly and tried to calm down. 'Paddy, are we going to your house?'

Beside her, Paddy shook her head vehemently. Again, came that long sentence that she could not interpret. She thought she made out the word 'secret' but could not be sure.

She was surprised when he took a track before the old farmhouse was reached and saw that he was heading to an old low barn apart from the other big barns.

Now she was feeling interested, and all the previous fear had left her. She felt the confidence of the driver beside her and was totally gobsmacked at his expert handling of the jeep. Where did he learn to drive like that?

He pulled the jeep in behind the barn and unlocked the doors. They both got out and he led Claire to a door in the barn. He took out a key and unlocked it and went inside. Claire followed. He put on an electric light and she found herself in a deserted space, a few piles of hay lying in one corner and a few pieces of old rusty machinery lying in another. She looked in puzzlement at Paddy.

He beamed at her and pointed to the furthest corner. He led her over and pointed to a ring in the floor which he grabbed and pulled upwards. A trapdoor opened and she could see a wooden stairway leading down.

Paddy led the way and put on another light as he went. Claire crept down timidly, there was fear again, plucking at her heart which had started beating fast.

At the end of the stairway, they were standing in a room about half the size of the upstairs barn floor.

Paddy beckoned her over and put on another light. Now she could see a furnished room, complete with a bed, a chest of drawers and a wardrobe.

Everywhere were boxes one on top of another, not very big boxes but bigger than shoe boxes.

Paddy went over and opened the wardrobe and smiled at her and pointed into it.

Claire stood beside him and saw a rail of women's clothing arranged neatly on hangers, beneath were several pairs of women's shoes all neatly paired, she could see a discrepancy: one shoe had no partner and she recognised it. Her heart began its rapid beating again. It felt like it was trying to escape like a bird caught in a cage or trap. She tried to calm her breathing and looked at Paddy. He had turned away and now went over to a chest of drawers and opened the top one.

Claire approached wordlessly, and numbly looked into the open drawer. Paddy nodded to her and said that word again that sounded like 'secret'. She gazed into a drawer full of mobile phones, some she recognised as outdated and old.

Paddy took one up and began pressing the numbers and putting the phone to his ear. Smiling, he offered it to Claire. It was flat and there was not a peep out of it. She looked desperately through them and then spotted one like Nessa had. She grabbed it and dialled her own number, she listened intently and willed it to ring but there was nothing.

Knowledge was building up in her brain and she knew that these phones had all belonged to different women at different times. She looked and saw a fairly modern version. She took it up and dialled Niall's number, which she knew off by heart. It rang and his message minder came on. She whispered a quick message, then rang Andy. She slumped in relief when she heard Andy's voice. Before she could say anything, Paddy had grabbed the phone from her and put it back. His face looked shocked, and he appeared to be frozen in place. Then he put his finger on his lips and whispered 'Ce'h shh, Monnacom.'

Swiftly for one of his size he pulled her over to the wardrobe and pushed her inside, closing the door.

She was suddenly full of energy and opened the door to step out when she heard the shouting.

'Paddy I know you're down there and I'm gonna beat the shit outta yah. I told you before, this is my room, not yours.'

She recognised Mick's voice and stepped back into the wardrobe in panic. What should she do; come out and laugh it off or stay and see what happens? Her brain stopped functioning then when she heard Paddy whimper.

The thuds and noises that ensued told her that Mick was beating Paddy who said nothing but whimpered and pleaded, 'Stoh Mih'.

She could bear it no longer and made to push open the door, but something stopped her, and she had a strong feeling that Nessa was holding her back.

The thuds stopped, she heard Paddy whimpering and Mick panting. Then there was another sound. Someone was coming down those wooden stairs and her heart leapt in joy and relief.

Then she heard Margie shouting at Mick.

'I told you before, he's a child. What have you hit him for? I thought I told you to get all this stuff out of here and get rid of it. Are you stupid or what?'

'This is my place, and I told the moron before, to keep out. It's private and for me only.'

'Nothing here belongs to you and you are the moron. If you ever touch him again, I'll...'

She was interrupted by Mick, 'you'll what? Call the guards?' He laughed harshly. 'Will you now sister? Just remember, you were glad of my services before, in dispatching your husband, you cannot say anything, or I'll spill the beans. And, don't forget, that it was you who brought Betty to me. Thought she would change her mind about settling here with me, did you? Well, we know how that turned out, don't we, so you were involved there too.

'I never told you to get rid of her, I wanted her to stay with you, at least it might have stopped your roaming around after girls.'

Mick laughed again, 'what do they say about a woman scorned? I soon tired of you Margie; you lost your appeal once you got pregnant, silly cow. You were grand before you had *him,* we had a perfect life, didn't we, once the parents were out of it. It was you suggested I come and work for Hugh. What a shock you must have got when I returned from England and went back to live in the cottage. So near you, yet so far away and you married. The old itch returned, didn't it? Then you became too obsessed with the baby, didn't you? The little monster!'

'That's rich, coming from you; just remember, he's your monster too, Mick. Come on Paddy, come home with Ma.'

Paddy whimpered again. 'Pa'h zori Ma'h, Pa'h a gudboynah. Mi'h, hima mona.'

Chapter 32

Niall was weary and his heart heavy. He came into the cottage and only when he was at the sink filling the kettle, did he realise the door had been left open. He called to Claire and getting no reply stopped and looked at his watch. It was one o'clock, the girl was probably fast asleep. Why did she leave the door open? She must have forgotten to lock it and it blew open with the wind. He drank a cup of tea and took a couple of painkillers for the headache that had bothered him all day then he went to bed after locking the door.

He was wakened it seemed like only moments later with a loud banging on the front door and then the back door. He was half asleep on his feet when he opened it and found Detective Savage and another guard on the step. They both pushed inside.

He was told to dress fast and was presented with a cup of coffee when he emerged from the bedroom. The young guard was coming down the stairs shaking his head.

'Claire is missing, Niall. Her bed is unslept in. Do you know where she is?'

Niall felt the blood draining from his face and sat down at the table. 'Oh, my God! The door was open when I returned and I never thought to look, I thought it just blew open in the wind.' He put his head in his hands.

Aidan put his hand on Niall's shoulder. 'We don't have time to sit and weep, lad. The good news is that a signal came from the latest victim's phone a couple of hours ago in the same area as the other two. Let's go and call in on Andy before we do anything else.'

As the men drew near the village, Niall checked his phone and saw the message from a strange phone.

He pressed the button and heard Claire's whispered message and could also hear the fear in her voice.

'Niall I'm up at the farm with Paddy, help me.'

He was going to redial it when he thought better and showed the phone to the detective.

'That's the mobile number of the latest victim, I think.' He was on the phone straight away to the investigating team and early as it was, there was someone on duty. He confirmed the number as being the newest victim.

'No don't redial it, we don't want to attract attention to that phone. Here we are, let's see if we can rouse Andy at this hour.'

Andy was still in bed as were his parents. At the continued hammering at the door, Andy appeared, followed by his mother. They were alarmed to see the guards so early in the morning.

Andy was not so alarmed as Niall was. There must be a rational answer as to why Claire rang him on a strange phone, but why she would be up on the farm he could not imagine. The guards said her car was still outside the cottage. How did she get up there then? Andy was told to dress quickly and come with them. Mary looked anguished as they left. What was going on, she wondered? She decided to say nothing to her husband, he was due at the hospital this afternoon and Andy had been due to stay at home today and do deliveries. Now what could she do?

As they sped towards the farm entrance off the main road, Niall asked Andy whether he had ever seen Paddy handle the rifle that would be the normal weapon found on any farm. Andy was indignant at first, but sensing the seriousness of the guards, admitted that the lad did have a fascination for all things connected to the farm, the jeep, the tractor and had indeed been caught holding the rifle once by Margie, who ranted and raved at her brother for leaving it lying around his house.

The rain was coming down in torrents now and the track was becoming a quagmire. Detective Savage looked at Niall and was on the phone a moment later and requested armed back up, just in case. Aidan's phone rang immediately after that call. He was told another call had been made to the emergency department from the same mobile number. He decided not to relay that news to Niall.

Again, Andy felt helpless but angry at these people for thinking that Paddy had that sort of violence in him.

'He doesn't have the intelligence to even think like this, lads. I tell you he's a harmless individual.

'That's all well and good, but that phone message came to Niall's phone from a mobile phone that belonged to a recent murder victim. Claire was asking for help and said she was with Paddy at the farm.'

That quietened Andy. How could that be explained away? He now felt miserable and worried about Claire. He was attracted to the lively redhead but knew he probably would not have a hope in hell of attracting her. She was used to life in Dublin and had a great job too. Look how she had helped Paddy.

The car slewed across the track; its wheels embedded in soft mud. The men swore and got out to try to push the car forward. There was no hope of shifting it. There followed a flurry of phone calls for help.

'Come on lads, there's nothing for it but to walk the rest of the way. Andy felt sorry for the men, at least he had his working boots on and was used to this terrain, especially in winter.

Heads down against the driving rain and wind the four men set off, slipping and sliding at times in the liquid mud.

Chapter 33

Claire was crouched inside the wardrobe, frozen in fear. She could not now come out after hearing all that. What would happen? She waited and then as the shouting stopped, she heard the receding footsteps of Margie and Paddy She waited in hope for the third set of footsteps to follow. There was silence for a time, then she could hear Mick moving about. She heard his footsteps getting nearer to where she was hiding in fear. This was it; he was going to discover her, and she knew she was danger.

As the wardrobe door began to open, a mobile phone suddenly pinged and Mick immediately walked rapidly over to the chest of drawers. She could hear him rummaging about and cursing as he sought to find the mobile that was ringing. It stopped abruptly.

There followed the sound of items falling on the bed and she believed he was emptying the drawer out. There followed louder cursing, ranting and raving. The man was in the grip of a temper tantrum and was storming around the room, knocking the boxes as he did so.

Gradually he quietened and she heard the retreating footsteps going up the stairs and the door of the barn banging shut. Unable to move still, she waited slowly releasing her breath.

She gently opened the door of the wardrobe fully and looked around. The mobile phones were on a heap on the bed as she had suspected. Should she try and contact Niall again. She picked up the newest looking phone that had caught her interest before, then she realised Niall would be at the cottage and probably be asleep.

Silently she dialled 999 and waited, hoping against hope, her watch showed it was two forty-five. She waited for an answer; finally, an automated voice asked what department was wanted, press one for ambulance, two for…..

Then she heard the barn door open and stopped the call. He was coming back! She went back into the wardrobe as silently as possible, this time standing in the corner free from hanging clothes.

He was back in the bedroom area of the room and she could hear his fiddling around with the phones again and the rustle of plastic. He is getting rid of them, she thought. The sounds of more rustling and movements around the room ensued. She was willing him not to come near the wardrobe. Then that ringing sound of a mobile again. Suppose it was the emergency services checking back on the number she had used. Stupid, stupid, she told herself, of course they would check back! If he answered it, he would know at once that it had been used from here, recently. Silently she prayed that he would not answer it. The cursing began again, and she heard the rustling and the rushing footsteps once more ascending the stairs.

Now was her chance to try and creep out and escape from this hellish situation.

She got to the top of the stairs; he had left the barn light on. She crept slowly to the door and looked around wildly for a place to hide if he reappeared. There were no hiding places here, that old pile of hay would never conceal her, she continued to the door, scarcely daring to believe she was almost free. She pushed gently against the barn door then more firmly as it did not move, until realising that he had locked the door and she was not free. Disappointment and despair flooded her, and she felt tears coming. She looked around for something she could defend herself with, but there was nothing there at all that would serve as a weapon.

She crept back downstairs and looked around for a different hiding place. If he were now getting rid of stuff, the wardrobe would be next she knew. Under the stairs was a dark area and she quickly went to explore. It was a rather primitive bathroom, she found: a latrine type toilet and a bucket of water which was half full. The door was made of thin plywood and not straight or able to close properly. Would this be a safer place to hide? The door was already half-open. If she stood behind it when he came next, would he bother to come in? Her brain was trying to analyse so many things at once; he would definitely be returning, but what about sleep? Would he wait until daylight? Would Niall have retrieved her whispered message before he came back to finish the job of clearing out? So many questions were flooding through her mind. She had completely forgotten Paddy and Margie. Would Paddy tell his mother that she was there? If he did that, what would Margie's reaction be after Mick's accusation.

The silence dragged on and Claire felt so weary in mind and body. She sank down with her back to the wooden wall of the obviously home constructed staircase. The door was on her right. She would stay here now behind that door, although her head touched the step above, when she stood upright. For now, she would stay in this crouched position until she heard the barn door open, as she knew it would. She said a prayer that he would wait until daylight before coming back to clear the room out, but being November, the mornings would be dark until after nine. Please let Niall be in the village to get my message, please.

She felt her eyes closing despite her fear, the cold was penetrating her bones, she tried to stay awake.

Chapter 34

The four men finally reached the top of the track. Andy was leading the way and he passed the old farmhouse and on to the next turn off the track, which was now a broad area. They could see the old tractor and more bit of machinery lying around. There was no sign of the jeep, but Andy kept walking and they saw the bungalow ahead. There was a light in the kitchen. Andy rapped on the window and after several minutes the kitchen door opened, and Margie looked out. She could only see Andy in the dark and went in leaving the door open. As Andy entered with the three men after him, her face changed expression and she looked startled and scared.

Andy quietly told her that they needed to speak to Paddy urgently. She silently left the kitchen, and they could hear her calling her son and telling to come to the kitchen.

She nervously entered the kitchen and put on the kettle. She did not ask why they wanted Paddy, which Niall thought was strange.

The man entered after a few minutes. He had obviously thrown on a few clothes: a mismatched tracksuit bottoms and top and slippers.

When he saw Andy, he beamed at him and said 'Dee', then he noticed the other two men standing by the kitchen door and his smile faded.

'What happened your face, Paddy? It's black and blue.'

'He had a fall Andy, a bit of a fall but he's alright, aren't you love?' Margie stepped to stand beside him.

Paddy put a hand to his face and looked at Andy.

'Paddy, where is Claire, we need to find her quickly. We know that she came up here with you last night.'

Paddy nodded and turned a worried face to Niall and Aidan.

'Can you show us where she is Paddy? Aidan asked gently.

Paddy nodded and went to the kitchen door, putting on his wellingtons which were standing on one side.

'Put on your coat Paddy, it's cold out there,' urged Margie.

The procession of men set off and were surprised when he passed the old farmhouse but set off along the narrow track to a small barn, some way off.

Andy running to keep up, asked, 'are you sure she is here, Paddy?'

Paddy spoke a long sentence that Andy could not really understand, except something about a secret room.

Then, there was the jeep parked at the side of the barn. They found the barn door open and the light on inside. Silently the men crossed the barn floor, looking for signs of recent occupation. Paddy then pointed to the open trapdoor on the floor.

They could hear someone moving about down there and looked at each other. Andy whispered to Aidan, 'will I call her?'

Aidan shook his head and put his finger on his lips. 'We wait and see what happens, we don't want to cause a panic.'

He beckoned them all to one side, against the wall. They would not be visible behind the trapdoor and would see who emerged.

They did not have to wait too long. The sounds of heavy footstep coming up the stairs reached them, and two heavy black plastic bags were pushed out. The person then went back down the stairs. Seconds later more plastic bags were pushed out, followed by the figure of Mick. Andy could feel Paddy freeze beside him, and he backed away further away from the scene.

Mick emerged fully now, and as he bent to pick up the two bags, he gasped in shock, as he saw the two guards approaching him.

'What's going on? Why are you here?'

'We are the ones who will be asking the questions, Mick. What exactly have you got there in those bags?'

'I'm finally clearing out Paddy's den or playroom, as his mother called it. Years of accumulated rubbish.'

'You won't mind us having a look then, will you? Aidan and Niall stepped forward and emptied out one of the bags. A pile of female clothing fell out then and in another bag was several pairs of lady's shoes.

'What's this then? Does Paddy like cross-dressing, Mick?' Andy stooped and looked at the shoes.

'Your guess is as good as mine. His mother suspects that something is not quite right with the lad.'

Then Paddy came forward and looked at Mick. 'Monna, ya'monna!' He dashed forward and went down the stairs rapidly. 'Ce'h, Ce'h, newawnrih?'

Mick, meanwhile, stood staring at the opening in the floor.

'There you go, he is away with the fairies, most of the time, so he is. Why does he think Claire is down there?' He laughed mirthlessly.

Niall shouted loudly, 'if you're there Claire, it's safe to come up. The guards have the place surrounded and Aidan and Andy are here too.'

They heard Claire's voice then, it was more of a sobbing sound and that of Paddy's, almost tender tone, as he soothed the distressed girl.

Mick was looking slack-jawed now and shocked and his face was a sickly colour and shiny with perspiration.

'Well, hasn't she had the lucky escape if that madman brought her here. I'll warrant he is a psycho.'

Outside there was an armed group of guards ringing the area. Margie was at the barn door, clearly distressed and wringing her hands.

'My Paddy is an innocent child, he's not the sick one here.'

Paddy emerged then holding Claire by the hand. The girl was shaking. Paddy put his arm around her and made soothing sounds. 'Saw ri', Ce'h.'

Andy and Niall came to the distressed girl and ushered her out of the barn. Two guards stepped forward took hold of Paddy's arm and led him to the waiting police car, amid Margie's hysterical shrieks.

Chapter 35

In the hours that followed a story emerged that began a long time ago. Claire recovered rapidly and urgently requested to be brought to the station where Paddy was being held. Andy accompanied her after seeing his aunt being put into an ambulance. Margie had suffered some sort of turn; they did not know whether it was a heart attack or stroke.

Mick was asked to attend a local station for questioning. He went willing and kept gushing on about how he knew that his nephew was not right and had asked his sister to see to him years ago.

Detective Inspector Aidan Savage and another detective interviewed Claire and Andy in a small informal room. It was not so much an interview as getting Claire to relate all that had happened her in the previous hours.

When she told them of Paddy taking her forcefully in the jeep, they looked at each other. She hastened to explain that the man had been desperate for her to understand about her friend and her car. She emphasised that she was not in danger from Paddy.

'It would seem from what I heard when I was hiding in the wardrobe that Mick is the father of Paddy.'

This stunned all three men in the room. Andy shook his head, 'but she was married to my uncle

Hugh, my mother was godmother to Paddy. That's just not possible Claire.'

'I'm just saying what I heard, Andy. She said that Paddy was his monster too when Mick called him that name.'

'That might have just meant that he was also responsible for how he turned out, seeing that his father was dead since he was a baby.' Aidan said this thoughtfully and the other detective nodded.

Claire put up her hand. 'Stop, I have just remembered something that Mary told me She had never told anybody and did not want her husband to know. She said that Hugh told his wife, Margie, that the baby was not his. He was very unhappy the poor man and died about six months after this.'

Niall and Aidan looked at each other. 'This throws a new light on things,' Aidan said. 'Could Mick be the father?'

'Well, when I was a child, Mick lived in the bungalow and I don't know when he moved to the old farmhouse. I never thought about it, to tell the truth. I know that Margie and Mick were not full siblings, he was her stepbrother. Both their parents got married having been widowed and both had a child each. They would have grown up together from the time they were about eleven or twelve.'

Andy was desperate to show these men that his cousin was no pervert and could have had nothing to do with all those items in the plastic bags that had been spilled out on the floor of the barn.

'Look, he has the mental capacity of an eight or nine-year old. Just because he grabbed Claire and was able to drive that jeep means nothing. He was able to drive the tractor, unknown to his mother. Mick knew though, we often needed him to drive when we were cutting the turf.'

Claire asked if they could see Paddy who must be so frightened by himself. They were told that he was fine, having chocolate biscuits and playing with a woman who worked in the police department. He was having great fun with the drawing materials and paper they provided him with.

Claire smiled at this and visibly relaxed.

'Now it was his drawings that alerted us to the missing car, we feel that he holds the key to this. What do you think Andy?' Niall asked this because he knew it was true.

It was Claire who answered that question. 'Of course he does, that was why he made me come with him. He wanted to show me but while showing me the mobile phones and clothes he heard Mick coming and pushed me into the wardrobe. He was terrified. Then Mick proceeded to beat him up., It was awful, and I was afraid to come out and help him. The poor lad was whimpering, and it went on until Margie appeared. They then started to accuse each other of things and Mick then said that it was she

225

who brought Betty to him, that's Elizabeth Cooney, the girl missing for over twenty-two years. Paddy was eight at that time.'

Claire paused for breath then and slumped back in the chair. She was exhausted but at the same time her heart was racing, and she knew they nearly had the problem solved.

It was Andy who galvanised them.

'Come on, let's go back to the farm and bring Paddy and see what he can tell or show us, please lads, this is important.'

Paddy was brought in thirty minutes later, beaming all over. Far from being cowed or frightened he was happy and was clutching a bag of new colouring materials and a bag of sweets.

The sun was shining weakly now and blue sky had replaced the darkness they had left in, earlier as they again travelled up to the farm.

Paddy understood that they were looking for the car belonging to Claire's friend and nodded excitedly at Andy.

They reached the small barn where the jeep was parked and the five of them transferred to that; it was a better vehicle for the bogland. The two men followed in the van.

It was exactly as the old print showed; a beautiful stretch of land, hilly in parts and then dropping to a valley backed by a mountain, with visible waterfalls flowing down into a lake. The brown earth showed the bog that was all around here, and some areas that showed recent cutting. There were heaps of sods left in places for drying.

They stopped on a level patch of land which looked down on the lake. Paddy got agitated then as they got out and started on his long rambling sentences that neither Claire nor Andy could understand.

Andy stopped him midstream. 'Paddy where is the car, you know, the one you always draw and the one in the painting?'

Paddy started walking forward rapidly, and the others followed him. He descended a steep slope and stopped. Everyone stood still and looked at him. Then he pointed to the lake and a long, garbled sentence issued forth as he pointed and waved his hand down at the black water.

Aidan and Niall looked down and then asked Paddy if he meant that the car was in the lake?

'Ess, ess, ca'r deh anmonnaputder.'

He was smiling and beaming at them. At last, they understood what he had been trying to communicate for such a long time.

Andy stood beside Paddy and asked him quietly, 'did you see Mick putting it there, Paddy?'

Paddy nodded, then put his finger on his lips, 'shh Pa'h see monna, monna no see Pa'h, no.'

Detective Savage was on his mobile to Killarney. There would be divers sent within a couple of hours and there would be machinery on hand. The man felt that they were on the right path and he put his hand sympathetically on Niall's shoulder. He suspected they were at the end of a sad and horrific story.

Niall also gazed down into the black waters. His beautiful sister was there, down in those dark depths, he felt sure of it. How could this have happened? He saw an image of his strong-willed sister; so talented and independent; sensible, if slightly eccentric.

Claire stood beside him and put her arm around him. She also knew in her heart that it was true, her friend was down there. It was as if they could feel her spirit around them, as if it were hovering here, in the still and silent air.

In the coming weeks and perhaps months, no one would be allowed to set foot in the place, neither here at the lake or the farmhouse. The entrances to the farm would be sealed off.

Chapter 36

The village of Kilshee was buzzing with the latest news. People heard bits and pieces, but they had not heard the whole story, not just then. The farm of Margie Cooney was completely sealed off, she was in hospital recovering from a heart complaint.

Andy and Paddy moved to the Lake Cottage and Claire returned home at last She needed time to be with her family and recover from the trauma she had suffered at being in the barn with a murderer and a little later to learn that the body of her dear friend Nessa had been recovered in her car, which had been lifted from the lake.

There were now fresh discoveries being made both in the lake and in the bog up by the lake. The remains of several missing people had been discovered including that of Elizabeth who was quickly identified by a cross and chain that her father had given her. Identification would now begin on all the other remains. and would be a lengthy process. DNA was being collected from relatives of all previously missing persons. It would be a grim job for all concerned.

Niall called to see Claire in Dublin and gave her the latest news. He was now removed from the enquiry and was trying to come to terms with the loss of

Nessa as were his family and Claire. A funeral would soon follow.

Mick had been charged with the murders of Nessa, and Elizabeth but the true numbers of other murders had not yet been ascertained. Margie was recovering in hospital and the detectives did not know if she would be charged with murder or complicity.

Mary had spent time with Claire before she left for home. She was relieved in a way, when the girl told her that Hugh had not committed suicide. How he met his death was now being investigated separately to the other murder investigations.

Claire had told Niall and Aidan about the exchange between Mick and Margie. She had not mentioned that accusation to Mary, wanting to spare the woman. She had enough on her plate with her husband in hospital recovering from a triple-bypass operation.

Hugh's death would now have to be dealt with. The detective hoped that Margie would be the one to cooperate. Mick was a psychiatric case they felt, a vicious and manipulative psychopath who deliberately had sought out lone women.

Andy and Paddy were allowed access to the barns where the ewes would soon be giving birth and they worked flat out every day, coming back to the cottage at night. The normality of the work helped Andy to forget about the other activities taking place further up by the lake.

It was during this time that a letter from a solicitor reached Andy. His mother gave it to him when he called to the shop on the way to the farm as he did every morning. On opening it, he discovered that he was now the owner of the farm where he had worked for the past four years. It was a bitter sort of pill for him to swallow. He put it away in the drawer under the counter and told his mother he would sit and talk about it some evening. It slowly dawned on him that he was now Paddy's guardian, in the event of Margie's death. He felt anger too; such a burden for a young man, without being consulted.

As the months passed the village once more became the quiet backwater that it always was. The satisfied media had long departed and besides, there were other murders and scandals to investigate.

It was the end of summer, twelve months later when Claire drove to Kilshee to see Mary and Joe and to spend time with Paddy and Andy. She had found a special school near Killarney that helped autistic adults and had been in touch with Andy. Margie was no longer living at the farm. She was being held in a women's prison up in a border county. Her trial was due to take place early in the new year when the other trials were finished.

Claire looked forward to seeing them all and had booked the cottage which had been empty all year.

She found Joe behind his counter as usual looking in good health. His colour was a lot better although his hair was completely white now. Mary was her usual self and was delighted to see the girl. She told Claire that Paddy was now attending the adult classes three times a week and loved it. His speech was improving a lot and it was easier to understand him now. Of course, she said, he was still a child and always would be. He did not seem to be missing his mother or Mick, she added wryly.

They did not dwell on the morbid happenings at the farm. Some things were better left not spoken about.

Claire looked forward to seeing Andy and Paddy later that evening. They were both back in the bungalow at the farm. Mary had said how strange it was that her family home was now back in their possession.

'Is Andy content with his lot in life then? Not hankering after New Zealand?'

'It's hard to say Claire. He loves the work up there and takes his responsibility to Paddy very seriously. As a mother, I don't know what to make of it, to tell you the truth. If he's happy then I am too, and his father. At least we get up there a lot and spend time with them.'

It was nine o'clock that night when Paddy and Andy arrived, bearing flowers and chocolates. Paddy was so excited, just like a child and started his long sentences before Andy stopped him.

'Now Paddy, what must you do? What did the teacher tell you?'

'Pa'hee mun sloh dowh, a lo'h. 'Ello C'hruh, we aw mistou.' Then he gave Claire a great bear hug.

Andy looked seriously at Claire. 'How is the sleuth doing? Did you miss us and all that excitement?'

He offered his hand, and she took it smiling and then hugged him tightly. 'I did indeed Andy, but the excitement I would not want again, ever.'

'It's good to see you back, I didn't think you would ever wish to see this place again, after all you have been through.'

'Well now, Andy and Paddy, you might be seeing a lot more of me,' she grinned mischievously at them.

Andy nudged Paddy and raised his eyebrows.

'Tomorrow I have an interview for a job in St. Ita's school, where Paddy is attending. I have completed a course in assistant teaching for adults and I decided a long time ago, that I've had enough of cities and this place has everything that is good, now that all the darkness and wickedness is gone. So now, who'd like a cup of tea and a chocolate bar?'

Printed in Great Britain
by Amazon